MW01088210

Betting

on a

Hot

SEAL

HOT SEALS

Cat Johnson

Copyright © 2017 Cat Johnson

All rights reserved.

ISBN-13: 978-1539533153
ISBN-10: 1539533158

CHAPTER ONE

"Hey, Dawson. Bet you a hundred bucks you can't eat that whole pizza in under five minutes."

"Dude, why would I want to do that?" Craig Dawson frowned at Bill Tompkins, the SEAL sitting opposite him.

Tompkins drew back. "What the hell kind of a question is that? It's Vegas. You gotta gamble."

If Craig wanted to gamble he could play the slots rather than make himself sick and ruin his meal. It wasn't like there weren't slot machines absolutely everywhere, from the gates at the airport to the grocery stores.

He couldn't even get to his hotel room without being led through the maze of gambling opportunities. It felt as if he'd covered miles just trying to walk from point A to point B this weekend because there was no direct path anywhere. But that, he supposed, was Vegas.

"I'm not a big gambler." Craig lifted one shoulder and bit into a piping hot slice of pizza, taking his time to savor the flavor.

It was good—thin crust, tasty sauce, not too much cheese, just the right amount of grease. Good pizza was something he could appreciate and something that was damn hard to come by outside of New York State where he'd grown up.

"But it's Vegas." Tompkins repeated himself, as if that fact would convince Craig to change his mind and take the ridiculous bet.

"Yup, it is." He nodded.

Training in Nevada definitely had a few perks. The proximity to twenty-four hour fun was one of them.

Last time they'd been aboard Naval Air Station Fallon the team had gone to Reno seeking entertainment since it was only an hour away from the air station.

This time, during the weekend liberty the team had been granted, they'd decided to take the trip to Sin City itself—Las Vegas.

There were many opportunities for entertainment there besides gambling, one of which Craig was very excited to take advantage of.

"So what are you going to do while you're here if not gamble? Take in the Celine Dion show?" Tompkins scoffed.

"Nope." Craig pulled a printed color brochure out of the back pocket of his pants and tossed it on the table. "That's what I'll be doing tomorrow."

Tompkins might be jonesing to gamble on anything and everything this weekend, but Craig had a different plan for his money. It was better than shows or even showgirls. Definitely better than sitting at a slot machine or a blackjack table in a sunless casino for hours.

The Adventure Range. He and a couple of his teammates were heading there tomorrow.

"A shooting range?" Tompkins frowned, staring at the brochure in his hand.

"Not just any shooting range. They take you in a helicopter over the Hoover Dam and the Grand Canyon, then you get dropped off to ride ATVs to the shooting range."

The furrow in Tompkins' forehead deepened. "This crap costs hundreds of dollars."

"Yeah, but it's almost a full day and you get a lot for that. And they feed you. At the end there's a barbecue with hamburgers and hot dogs."

Tompkins cocked one brow high. "Did you get brain damage during your last op? You do remember what you do for a living, right? Pretty much all of this stuff and the Navy pays *you* to do it, not the other way around."

"But that's work. This is for fun. And we've got a bet riding on who's the best shot." Craig figured Tompkins would appreciate that at least, since he seemed to be ready to bet on just about anything, including eating pizza.

Tompkins rolled his eyes. "You're nuts."

"If I am, then so is the rest of my team because a bunch of us are going. Brody Cassidy wants to check it out since his brother Chris is thinking about opening something similar back home."

"Fine." Tompkins tossed the brochure onto the table. "Anyway, that bullshit is tomorrow. Right? You can still go out and have fun tonight."

Craig swallowed another bite of pizza and shrugged. "I guess. As long as I'm not home too late."

He didn't want to be tired for the big day since he had a hundred bucks riding on this bet with his teammates about who could score best on the range tomorrow. But besides the money, there was his pride.

Craig would be damned if the older guys bested him. They treated him like a kid already. And it seemed no matter how many months passed and how many missions he went on with them, he was still considered a new guy by the others who'd been on this team for years.

No matter how well he performed during missions he would always have years less in the field than the older guys. At least until they retired and he became *the old guy*.

He couldn't seem to combat the image. Even more than a year after Craig had finished training and been accepted into the elite DEVGRU program and been assigned to his team they still called him *the kid*. Craig feared it was now his nickname, whether he liked it or not.

Maybe when someone younger joined the team it would change. But for now—at the Adventure Range—*there* he'd be on equal footing. He intended to take full advantage of it.

He couldn't wait.

Although, Tompkins was right. Craig could have a little bit of fun tonight and still be sharp for the range tomorrow.

Hell, more than a bit of his training prepared him

to function at peak performance on little-to-no sleep.

"What are you planning on doing after you finish eating that?" Craig tipped his chin to indicate the single oversized meatball on Tompkins' plate.

The thing was the size of a baby's head. He'd never seen a meatball that giant before in his life. It was a little freaky.

No wonder his teammate Rocky Mangiano had turned up his nose at this restaurant. Rocky, a born and bred connoisseur of Italian cuisine, had sneered and called it *tourist food.*

Looking at the plate in front of his dining partner, Craig had to admit the meatball sure didn't look like something Rocky's mother would serve up at home.

As Tompkins attacked the beast of a ball with fork and knife, he said, "I'm hitting up a bar."

"A bar?" Now it was Craig's turn to scoff. "You can go to a bar at home."

"First off, there are slot machines in the bars here, which there aren't at home. Second, this particular bar happens to be strategically right outside the theater and directly in the path of the women leaving the male strip show, which gets out . . ." He referred to the watch on his left wrist. "In two hours."

The reason for Tompkins' excitement about the bar was becoming clearer to Craig. "Ah, gotcha. You going alone?"

"Nah. I'm meeting a couple of the guys from my unit there but you're more than welcome to join us."

Tompkins was on a different assault team than

Craig, but they were all part of the same line squadron and overseen by the US Naval Special Warfare Command.

This Tier One special mission counter terrorism unit—what the media still referred to as SEAL Team Six even though the name was no longer technically correct—was currently away from their home base in Virginia and in Nevada for training.

Rather than hang out alone, or go back to his hotel room, he figured he could spend an hour or two with Tompkins and the other guys joining him.

Craig nodded. "All right. Thanks. I think I will come for a little while."

Enjoying a drink while watching Tompkins and his teammates hitting on a hoard of women horny from the all-male show they'd just seen? Yeah, that could definitely make for an entertaining, not to mention amusing evening.

CHAPTER TWO

Mary Elizabeth Smith stared at her reflection in the full-length mirror hanging on the back of the door in her bedroom and sighed.

Dressed in high heels and a black pencil skirt with a wine-colored blouse she looked okay. Good, even.

Sure, she'd worn this outfit to work today but it was appropriate to go out in too. She'd thrown on bigger earrings and a chunky bracelet, pulled her shoulder-length brown hair out of the bun she'd worn it in all day and she looked ready to go out with the girls.

So why was she worrying? Probably because she knew her friends would be so dressed up compared to her, she'd look like their mother. Or a teacher. Which she was, so there might be no avoiding that.

Looking ready wasn't really the issue. The problem was she'd far rather stay home tonight.

Her girlfriends—one married, one single—didn't seem to understand that. She'd managed to beg out of their weekly girls' night out for months now, but all of the usual excuses didn't work this time.

For some reason her friends had taken it on as their single goal this week to drag her out with them.

And to a male strip show too.

What the hell was that about? For a bachelorette party, or for a birthday celebration, it would be fine. But this was just a normal Friday night.

This was one of the hazards of living in the Vegas area, she supposed. Everything was over the top here, even girls' night out.

If she didn't have a really good job at UNLV, she'd relocate, but it wasn't like there was a whole lot of opportunity for someone in her area of study. She probably should have considered that before getting an advanced degree in Art History specializing in rare antiquities.

Lesson learned.

With another sigh, she turned away from the mirror.

Shoulders slumping, she felt like she had the energy of a sloth as she moved to the closet to find a small purse to carry for the night in exchange for her oversized tote she used every other day. Her life was in that bag and she hated the idea of going out without it, but it would be crazy to carry and try to keep track of it all night long.

If she knew one thing it was that the evening wouldn't end with the show. Her girlfriends would drag her to a bar afterward where she'd have to smile and pretend to enjoy herself while nursing overpriced drinks and watching her friends flirt.

Mary Elizabeth had just transferred her phone, money, identification, lipstick and travel-sized bottle of painkiller—because no doubt she'd need it for the headache this night would bring—into her small black bag when her cell phone rang.

The display showed it was Amanda, one of the two women forcing her to leave her house at night when she'd rather be in her pajamas watching television.

Reluctantly, Mary Elizabeth hit to answer the call. Cradling the cell on one shoulder as she clipped her clutch shut, she said, "Hello."

"Hi. Are you on your way?"

"Um, almost."

"You're not in the car yet?"

"No." Mary Elizabeth cringed and walked toward the kitchen in hopes of finding her car keys there.

"You're going to be late." The panic in Amanda's tone increased.

"No, I won't. I'll be fine." Although the traffic getting to a hotel on the Vegas Strip might be bad this time of night on a Friday. Just another reason to stay home . . . "If I am late, just go in without me."

"But I have your ticket. Mary Elizabeth! You had better not be planning on ditching us." Amanda using her full name made it feel too much like her friend was her mother and she was a kid again and in trouble.

Mary Elizabeth stifled a sigh. "I'm not."

"I don't believe you. You've become a complete

shut in since Rob broke up with you. You never want to do anything. You're life is not over. You have to get out. Meet someone new."

Just the sound of his name caused a familiar ache in Mary Elizabeth's chest. She'd gotten used to the pain, but not over it.

The feeling of sadness, of loneliness, was simply the new normal. After all these many months it was duller, less sharp, but still ever present.

With the hurt still fresh as a reminder of what havoc love could do to a woman, the last thing she was going to do was open herself up to that kind of pain again with someone new.

Why did her friends think jumping into a relationship with a new man could help? That would be like nearly drowning in the undertow and then diving right back into the water thinking this time would work out better.

No. No more men. At least not for a good long while.

The sudden, completely unexpected end of a nearly eight year long relationship should take a while to get over. And she was getting over it, in her own way, in her own time, by herself privately . . . except for tonight when she had let her friends sway her into going out.

Mary Elizabeth drew in a breath and felt the tightness in her chest that thinking of him—or rather the loss of him—had caused.

"I promise you, Amanda, I'm walking out the door right now."

Or she would be as soon as the elusive car keys presented themselves to her.

She flipped on the overhead light and finally spotted the keys next to the cell phone charger dangling from the wall in the corner of the counter. She swiped them up and turned toward the door.

"You'd better be. Jenny and I will be waiting for you right outside the door."

"All right. See you in twenty minutes."

"You'd better."

"I will. Goodbye." Mary Elizabeth hit the screen to disconnect the call before Amanda lectured her some more.

Well-meaning friends might just be the death of her.

They didn't understand that painful memories of that relationship were everywhere.

In the eight years worth of photos occupying half the space in her cloud storage account.

Woven into the clothes in her closet as she remembered wearing each outfit with him. Hiding in her lingerie drawer in the form of the sexy matching bras and panties he'd given her each year for Valentines Day.

In the fact the anniversary of the date they met was her password for every damn one of her devices.

In the unfinished game in the Scrabble app on her tablet.

At the beginning, even using her stupid toothbrush was painful as she remembered buying it while they were grocery shopping together. She'd thrown that one out and bought a new one, but seeing the replacement twice a day when she opened the medicine cabinet inevitably brought to mind the memory of the old one she'd tossed . . . and of how he'd tossed away both her and their life together.

Mostly the pain was a daily reminder of the fact she now lived in an apartment she'd never wanted because she had sold her condo to get the cash to put a down payment on a house they had found and fell in love with together.

It was to be their forever home. The place they'd spend their future together. *Forever* ended when he broke up with her right before the closing date leaving her out the deposit and basically homeless since she'd had to vacate the condo she'd sold.

Her friends needed to understand that people were different. They healed in different ways. Recovered at different rates. Had different comfort levels.

When Jenny broke up with her boyfriend, she got over it by going out every night with Amanda— though married—acting as wing-woman.

That was fine with Amanda because she hated being at home even though it was a beautiful house and she was in a happy marriage. She just didn't have it in her to sit still for too long so she went out as often as possible with Jenny. Luckily, Amanda's husband worked nights and didn't mind her not being home.

Mary Elizabeth mourned the loss of the relationship as if she was grieving an actual death. She couldn't bounce back like Jenny had. Couldn't go out nightly like Amanda loved to do.

She was the complete opposite in almost every way yet she and Amanda and Jenny were friends and had been for half of their lives. That either spoke to the truth behind the saying that opposites attract, or to the fact that Mary Elizabeth was too anti-social to make new friends.

As she battled the traffic, she decided not to beat herself up about it. She needed all her energy for the night of *fun* ahead.

A male strip show. Honestly! What made her friends want to see that? Those shows were for the tourists, not the Nevada locals . . . and perhaps Mary Elizabeth was as much of a stick in the mud as her friends accused her of being.

At least during the show, unlike at the bar, all the men would be on stage and she could safely sit in the dark and observe the whole carnival.

Her dread of the night ahead pressed like a physical weight on her chest, nestling in nicely next to the tightness she'd grown accustomed to since the breakup.

The lights of the strip came into view. Mary Elizabeth had to admit it was pretty. People traveled from all over the world just to see what she had right in her backyard.

Strangely the lights cheered her up a bit. She rallied and vowed to try to enjoy the night. As long as she had to go out, she should just try to have a good time.

Unfortunately, lately she'd become such a hermit she feared that was easier said than done.

CHAPTER THREE

Craig swirled the ice and amber liquid in his glass on the table, listening to the three SEALs from the other unit talk.

"Murphy's team is still over there going door to door. Block by block. Street by street. Taking back one neighborhood at a time."

"It's a slow process. It all looks the same when you're there in the shit. Sometimes the only way to see that we made any damn progress is by looking at the map in the war room."

"But there is progress in Mosul. We saw that when we were there. Every day the red area on the map gets a little smaller and the green zone increases."

"Yeah, but still, being back in Iraq, fighting for a city we'd already fought for, it was like we slipped in a fucking wormhole and went back in time to a decade ago."

"Back to when we took Fallujah."

"You mean when we took Fallujah *the first time*. Not to be confused with when we had to go back and retake it again last year."

"Kind of like taking Ramadi in oh-six, and then again in twenty-sixteen."

The two older guys from Tompkins' unit spoke mostly to each other, volleying the memories back and forth like a ball on a ping pong table.

"Except this time the man who's protecting your six is just as likely to be a foreign national as an American brother," Tompkins pointed out as he joined what had mostly been a two man discussion.

"Yeah." The guy they called Fitz for short nodded. "There is that. But I think after two years of ISIS rule, even us Americans are starting to look pretty good to the local army in comparison."

"*The enemy of my enemy is my friend,*" Clyde, the other older SEAL, quoted.

"Ain't that the truth?" Fitz laughed. "And thank God for it because with all the different factions fighting ISIS and fighting each other, it's getting hard to keep them all straight and know who to shoot."

"Except that we're only in Iraq as advisors. Right? No boots on the ground." Tompkins grinned and glanced around the table.

There were nods from the other two.

The talk of battles that these guys had personally fought back in 2006 kept Craig quiet. He wasn't about to remind them the only fighting he'd done that year had been on the playground in middle school.

For that fight he'd gotten dragged into the principal's office. These guys had taken fire and likely still carried the shrapnel. They'd lost friends and teammates. All he'd lost was recess privileges for a week.

He also felt the need to stay mostly quiet since he was the only one there not from the other unit. That really wasn't an issue, except in Craig's own mind. They'd welcomed him to join them when he'd shown up with Tompkins.

They all knew each other casually since his unit and theirs had trained together that week in the Nevada desert and the units worked together on occasion.

But he didn't have much to contribute to this particular conversation as two of the older teammates reminisced about the past.

They probably shouldn't be talking about this anyway, given where they were. The four of them—the two old timers, Craig and Tompkins—sat at a corner table and the noise from the casino surrounding the bar made the chance of anyone hearing them slim, but Craig still erred on the side of caution when discussing ops. Even ones that happened a decade ago.

"Hey. Looks like the show is letting out." Tompkins tipped his chin toward the public area outside the bar.

Craig twisted to look in the direction Tompkins had indicated and saw a steady stream of women being funneled between the slot machines and the brass rail that delineated the confines of the bar where they sat.

All chatty and animated, the women certainly looked as if they'd just been to the show in the theater located farther down this end of the building.

He turned back to face the table and said, "Doesn't mean they'll come in here."

"Oh, no?" Tompkins grinned. "Look again."

Craig didn't have to turn again and look to realize what Tompkins said was correct. The noise level around him had suddenly increased by a few decibels and it had a distinct feminine sound to it. Giggles. Squeals. And lots of scraping and shuffling as the ladies moved available chairs to empty tables, trying to create a spot of their own in the crowded bar.

He was glad the other guys had arrived early and claimed this area. From here they could observe everything happening from their out of the way corner.

"So, let's get down to it." Tompkins slapped a dime on the table and looked around at everyone seated there. "Dare for a Dime."

Craig lifted a brow. "Two hours ago you were trying to bet me a hundred dollars to eat a pizza. Now it's a dime? What happened? You lose all your money at one of the craps tables while I was in the men's room?"

Fitz let out a laugh. "That's very possible, I'm sure. But no, not in this case. Dare for a Dime is a team tradition. A game we play whenever we're out drinking."

"Sounds great." Laughing, Craig rolled his eyes.

A dime wouldn't get much nowadays. He was

pretty sure even gumball machines took quarters.

"Tompkins has the dime so he gets to choose the man and set the dare," Fitz explained. "Then, the guy who completes the dare gets the dime and the power to dare someone else."

Craig still wasn't all that impressed with the game. He supposed that showed in his expression since Clyde shook his head and said, "You gotta understand. It's not the value of the dime—"

"It's the valor of the dare," Fitz finished for his teammate.

"Exactly." Tompkins nodded and pushed the dime toward Craig. "So you're up, Dawson. This dare is yours."

Knowing Tompkins, Craig was a little concerned over what this dare might entail.

He really should have sucked it up and gone out with the guys from his own unit. They were out for an insanely expensive steak dinner at the restaurant inside The Palms. He couldn't bring himself to drop that much cash for a piece of steak he could probably grill better himself at home.

Now it seemed his frugality was going to cost him in other ways, unless he could get out of this dare.

He eyed the dime and grasped at his one chance for escape. "It's your team tradition. You guys should play. I don't want to butt in."

Clyde grinned and slid the dime closer to Craig. "Good try, kid, but no go. This one is all yours."

Now they were calling him *kid* too. He stifled a sigh regretting his choice to join them even more.

"And remember that after you complete your

challenge, you get to choose the dare and the man," Fitz reminded.

It might be worth it just to get revenge on Tompkins and teach him a lesson . . . *if* Craig could come up with a suitable challenge as punishment. He'd have to think about it, but until then he had a dare to complete.

Craig sighed and glanced toward Tompkins. "All right. Shoot. What's the dare?"

Tompkins grinned so wide Craig had to wonder if he'd just made a huge mistake.

CHAPTER FOUR

"Don't look now, but that table of guys is staring at us," Jenny said, looking more than happy about it.

"Really? Well, let's give them something to stare at then." With an evil smile, Amanda surreptitiously hiked her boobs higher while tugging her blouse a bit lower.

"Amanda!" Mary Elizabeth lost the battle with herself and glanced at the table of grinning men to see if they'd noticed that less than subtle move. She shielded her face with her hand and said, "Remember, you're married."

"I'm married, not dead."

"Amen to that. And I'm single, so . . ." Jenny shrugged.

Mary Elizabeth shook her head at her man-crazy friends. "What is happening with you two? You're not supposed to have your midlife crisis for at least twenty more years."

"What's wrong with accepting some positive male attention?" Amanda asked.

"And getting free drinks that men buy us is even better." Jenny smiled.

Mary Elizabeth wasn't sure male attention found in a bar in a casino was so positive, or that the free drinks would be worth dealing with it, but it was no use trying to change her friends' opinions. She knew they were good and set in their ways.

"I think the bigger question is what's happened to you, Mary Elizabeth? You're acting like you're in your sixties instead of in your thirties. You're single too, you know." Jenny cocked one brow high.

"Yes, I know." Mary Elizabeth didn't need Jenny's reminder of that or her heartbreak. The memory of it was firmly branded into her mind where it rose to taunt her each night as she lay sleepless in her bed.

Amanda covered Mary Elizabeth's hand with her own. "Why don't you go over and talk the them?"

Her eyes flew wide. "Are you crazy?"

"No. Are you? Look at them. Big and strong. Blonde. Dark. Young. Old. Taller. Shorter. It's like a man sampler at that table. There has to be at least one that you're interested in."

"They could all be married for all we know." That possibility was far from Mary Elizabeth's only objection but it was the best she could come up with at the moment.

She had to do something to subdue her friends, who she feared might just get up and drag those men over whether she liked it or not.

"And they might not be married. You won't know unless you talk to them," Jenny pointed out.

She shook her head. "It doesn't matter either way. I'm not looking for a relationship right now."

Amanda shrugged. "Then don't get into a relationship. Just enjoy the night."

"A one-night stand?" Mary Elizabeth squeaked. That was not her style.

"Why not?" Jenny asked. "We won't judge you."

Amanda nodded. "Of course, we won't. I think that's exactly what you need. Kind of a sexual palate cleanser to rid you of any remains of the last asshole and clear the way for the next serious man in your life."

Clearly her two friends had a coordinated plan all worked out to get her laid, whether Mary Elizabeth was willing or not. Short of leaving and going home, she didn't know what to do to get them off the topic of her love life or get out of their plan for hooking her up with random men.

Maybe that's exactly what she should do. Go home.

She'd fulfilled her responsibility and gone to the show, and had even joined them for a cocktail afterward. She should be able to leave now with a clear conscience.

Mary Elizabeth knew they'd fight her leaving. She was going to have to be strong and not let them sway her. But before she left she should hit the restroom since it could be a long ride home with traffic.

Pushing the remains of her drink away, she slid

her chair back. "I'm going to the ladies room."

Jenny downed the remains of her own drink and pushed the empty glass toward the center of the table. "As long as you're walking up there, can you tell the bartender to send over the cocktail waitress with another round?"

"Sure." Mary Elizabeth would do that, but she'd put in the order for only two insanely strong cocktails, not three.

How the hell her friends could down what amounted to straight chilled vodka was beyond her. She sure couldn't have more than one. Even finishing the one she'd had would put her in danger of not being able to drive safely or legally. Which is why she'd left half of it on the table.

Shaking her head at her friends' capacity for alcohol, and still not knowing how to get out of there without a fuss, Mary Elizabeth headed for the bar. Maybe a plan or excuse would present itself while she waited to get the bartender's attention.

She was standing, moderately patiently, waiting for the bartender to finish with the order he was currently making when she saw him out of the corner of her eye—the young one from the man buffet her friends had been so excited about.

The young one also turned out to be a big and tall one, dwarfing Mary Elizabeth's petite frame as he moved close—too close—and leaned his forearms against the edge of the bar right next to where she stood.

"Hey." He shot her what might be a charming smile if she were interested.

Which she wasn't, she reminded herself.

Mary Elizabeth cut him a sideways glance and noticed how attractive the shortly cropped blondish scruff on his chin was before dragging her gaze away. She didn't want to lead him on or give him the wrong impression.

"Hi." After the single word acknowledgment she went back to staring imploringly at the bartender in hopes he'd see her silent plea and come over. Then she could take care of what she was there to do and leave before the hot guy who'd addressed her decided to get too chatty.

"Can I buy you a drink?" he asked, his brown gaze on hers.

"Just getting myself a water, but thanks." She shot him a half-hearted smile and went back to her stalking of the bartender.

"Um, look, here's the deal. I don't want to bother you but my friends dared me to come over and talk to you. If I didn't do it, I would have never heard the end of it from them so I had to. I'm sorry."

Intrigued by his confession, Mary Elizabeth turned to face him. "They dared you just to talk to me?"

Adorably, he dropped his gaze as if embarrassed before bringing it back up to meet hers. "Actually, they dared me to do a little more than just talk."

"How much more?"

He hesitated and then sighed. "Tompkins wanted to actually see me kiss you, right here in the bar, but I told him no go. Fitz convinced him that if I got your number it should be good enough."

The depth of detail in his story, on top of his real or possibly fake shame at having to admit it, was intriguing.

She laughed. "Either you're the most honest man in this place, or this is your attempt at appearing that way just to pick me up. I can't decide."

He lifted a brow. "I'm not really sure what to do to convince you either way."

She extended her hand as an idea struck. "Mary Elizabeth Smith."

"Craig Dawson." He laughed as he shook her hand. "And I have to tell you that Mary Smith is possibly the worst fake name I've ever heard."

Now it was her turn to raise a brow at him. "Sorry, but believe it or not it's actually my name. I was named after my two grandmothers, Mary and Elizabeth."

She didn't miss how he was still holding her hand in his as he nodded and said, "I believe you."

"Do you?" she asked.

"Yup. The addition of the backstory about your grandmothers makes all the difference." He grinned.

"Good. And I think I believe your story too, Craig Dawson." Believe him or not, the handholding was becoming ridiculous. Mary Elizabeth disengaged herself from his grip.

He let her go, but didn't move away. "That's good to hear. So what do we do now?"

If they'd met at a time in her life when she wasn't broken, and if he had been another decade older, and if he was flirting with her at somewhere besides a casino bar on a dare, she might have been interested in this man. But as it stood, there were way too many points against them.

The circumstances might be completely wrong,

but there was still no reason why they couldn't help each other out of a sticky situation, which was exactly what her stroke of brilliance was about.

She had a plan.

Mary Elizabeth was more than ready to go home but her friends weren't going to let her leave—*unless* she left with this guy. She might be crazy, but she was going to do it. Ask him to help her if she helped him.

Without further thought that might have made her change her mind, she said, "How would you feel about helping me out with something in exchange for me helping you with your friends?"

He tipped his head. "I think I might be interested in learning more."

"Good. My nosy friends, who like to interfere in my life, are pushing me to meet men, whether I want to or not. Since you've got this dare with your friends and I've got to get my friends off my back, what do you say we kill two birds with one stone?"

A smile lit his handsome face. "Sure. What exactly did you have in mind?"

CHAPTER FIVE

It was an interesting turn of events. Craig wasn't sure exactly how it had happened, or what would happen next. All he knew was he was leaving with Mary Elizabeth Smith—if that was indeed her real name.

The dare would be complete and he would be the victor. He could leave without any razzing from the other team for skipping out early. And on top of it all, a hot woman was indebted to him. Not a bad outcome to this insane dime dare.

"So how exactly do we play this?" he asked her, wondering if her brown hair felt as soft as it looked.

"I'll go tell my friends and you'll go tell yours that we're leaving."

"Do we go over and tell them together or separately?" he asked.

Her pretty hazel eyes widened. "Oh no. Not together."

He laughed at her reaction. "Why not?"

She shook her head. "You don't know these women. They're relentless. You can't handle them and their interrogation."

Craig had been trained well to withstand interrogation. Torture too. He was pretty sure he could handle a couple of nosy girlfriends but he let it go.

Besides, it was smarter to not subject her to the guys at his table anyway, so it was better they both take their leave from their respective friends separately.

"All right. We go ditch the friends and meet up." He glanced around. "Over by the door to the restrooms, I guess?"

It was immediately across the hall from the bar area. Close but far enough to keep them clear of nosy friends as they made their escape out the door to the parking lot where he'd parked his rental car.

"All right." She nodded. "I'll be quick."

"Sounds good." Getting out of there fast was his preference too. But after that, once clear of his friends and hers, Craig would love to take things long and slow.

Who knew? Maybe things might work out after all. He'd hated Tompkins' little game but if it yielded him an unexpected connection to this woman, he'd be more than happy.

Maybe she'd agree to go somewhere else and have a drink with him.

Mary Elizabeth definitely wasn't what he'd expected to find in the pool of strip show attendees they'd have to pick from. She was sober—in both demeanor and consumption.

And the style of her clothes were as serious as she appeared. In the straight-laced skirt and blouse, she could easily walk into a board meeting or something and fit right in.

Not that what she had on was unattractive. Not at all. In fact, the outfit definitely leant itself to a few fantasies, such as his sitting her on top of a meeting room table, hiking that skirt up and having his way with her.

Yeah, right.

He could tell already she wasn't that type. If she had been, they wouldn't be faking a hook up. They'd be actually hooking up.

Oh, well.

Hands in his pockets, he strolled over to his table, knowing the eyes of the three guys there had never left him.

"So I didn't get her number." He pursed his lips together. "But I guess I can get it later. You know—after."

"After what?" Clyde asked.

Craig tipped his head toward the table of women. "She's just saying goodbye to her friends and then we're out of here."

"You're leaving with her?" Tompkins' eyes popped wide.

"Yup. I sure am."

Tompkins shook his head. "I don't believe it."

"Sorry, but it's true. Wanna follow us and make sure?" Craig laughed, knowing a show of confidence would be the best way to sell this lie.

Luckily, he saw Mary Elizabeth heading for the

bar exit. She shot him a glance before she descended the stairs that led from the bar to the main floor and their meeting spot.

"Gotta go. My lady awaits. Oh, and since I don't have time to think up a good enough dare for Tompkins right now, I'm giving the dime to Fitz. Can you come up with something suitable?" Craig asked him as he slid the coin across the table.

Fitz grinned. "I'll do my best."

"Great. Thanks. See you guys." Taking his leave before there were any more questions, Craig strode down the stairs and over to her.

The glance she sent him was troubled. "My friends are suspicious."

"I can't say I'm surprised. Mine are too. We probably should have dragged it out for a bit to make it seem more convincing." He moved a bit closer, trailing the back of his fingers down her arm while dipping his head low toward hers. "Think this will help any?"

She lifted her gaze to meet his. Her throat worked as she swallowed before she said, "It might."

It was certainly making things feel more real to him. Judging by the quickening of Mary Elizabeth's breathing, she felt it too.

He reached for her hand and laced his fingers through hers. "And this?"

She nodded. "Yes. Probably."

His gaze dropped to her lips, so temptingly close.

Damn. Keeping this hook up fake would be so much easier if she was a little less attractive. And if she didn't smell so good.

What was that scent? She smelled like sunshine and something else. Maybe the beach.

He dipped his head a little lower to get a better take on the enticing fragrance as he said, "We should go."

"Yeah." She didn't move. Neither did he.

If they didn't go soon he'd be kissing her, right there in the casino under the scrutiny of his friends and hers.

If he kissed her, he was going to like it. He knew it. Then he wouldn't want to stop and unless Mary Elizabeth had changed her mind, he would have to stop.

To hell with it. Nothing ventured, nothing gained.

"Maybe we'd better get rid of any leftover doubt first." He cupped her face in one palm.

She nodded. "Okay."

That was all the confirmation he needed to close the remaining distance between them.

After a moment of surprise, she was kissing him back, her lips warm and yielding as he pressed his mouth against hers.

Maybe he shouldn't have done it but he did anyway—he pulled her tighter against him, tipped his head to the side and kissed her deeper.

He half expected her to pull away. When she didn't he slid his tongue between her lips and plunged into the heat of her mouth.

Damn, he could happily do this with her all night. Doing more would be good too. He'd gladly be tired for the shooting range tomorrow if he could spend tonight with Mary Elizabeth.

But that wasn't going to happen because all too soon, she pulled back.

"Can we go?" she asked.

"Yeah. Of course." A small part of him held out hope that she wanted to leave so they could be alone somewhere—and naked—but the rational part of him knew better.

That was confirmed when she dropped his hand the moment they were clear of the exit and out of view of their friends.

He let her lead him to her parked car and stood by as she unlocked the door and tossed her purse inside. "So, um, thank you for helping with my getaway."

Resigned, he tipped his head. "You're welcome. And thank you for helping me save face with the whole dare thing."

Her lips tipped up in a smile. "No problem."

"So, any chance I could get your number?" It was a shot in the dark but still he had to take it.

"Craig." Mary Elizabeth shook her head. "I'm flattered. Really. But—"

"The answer is no. I get it." He drew in a breath and said, "So I guess a good night kiss is a no too?"

The joke was to lighten the mood. He wasn't sure it had exactly worked when she treated him to a small but somehow sad smile.

"It's not you. I'm just not interested in anything right now with anyone."

She was using the old *it's not you, it's me* excuse to let him down easy. But there was something in her eyes as she spoke that gave him the feeling there was more to her story. That it wasn't just a brush off.

It was pointless to ask her what it was though. They didn't know each other well enough for her to confide in him. He'd been shot down and he was man enough to deal with it.

Craig nodded is acceptance. "Understood. Well, thank you for an interesting and unexpected evening."

Her smile looked genuine as she laughed. "It certainly was that. Good night, Craig."

"Good night, Mary Elizabeth Smith. It was a pleasure meeting you."

"For me too." She shot him one last glance as she climbed into the car.

He swung her door shut and took a step back, waiting until she'd started the engine and pulled out of the space. When she waved goodbye he waved back and watched her taillights disappear when she turned out of the lot.

One day he could picture himself meeting a woman like Mary Elizabeth and falling head over heels. He wasn't sure he believed in love at first sight or soul mates and all that other bullshit.

But falling in love one day? Yeah, he could get on board with that.

It was obvious today was not that day. He pulled out his phone and turned toward where he'd parked. He texted the guys to confirm the meet-up time in the morning as he headed across the lot to the row where he'd left the rental car.

He might not have won the woman tonight, but he'd be damned if he didn't come out on top at the shooting range tomorrow.

CHAPTER SIX

"You're seriously not going to tell us what happened between you and the hot guy?" Amanda asked through the cell phone.

"Nope."

"But we're your best friends."

"Yes, you are."

Amanda let out a huff. "I can't believe it."

Mary Elizabeth laughed. "Well, believe it. I don't kiss and tell."

The worst part was, there actually had been a kiss. A good kiss. A kiss that at another time in her life she would have really enjoyed.

But no, she could not—would not—let her head be turned by a handsome man with talented lips.

Men made promises and then broke them. Men gave you hope and then yanked it out from under your feet. Men vowed to stay and then they abandoned you, leaving you to clean up the mess they made of your life all alone.

Men sucked . . . and yet she still suffered from the loss of one of them.

He didn't deserve that. Though, no, maybe it wasn't the loss of Rob but rather the end of the relationship that she mourned.

The ending of it had felt like going through the death of a loved one. She'd gone through all the stages of grief.

Months later, she still felt the loss, so keenly she had no interest in any other men or the emotional entanglements that came with them.

So, strike one against the handsome and sexy Craig Dawson was that he was a man and she didn't want another one of those right now—if ever.

Strike two, who knew where Craig and his hot and talented mouth came from? This was Vegas. Tourists traveled there from far and wide. He could live thousands of miles away.

She didn't want any relationship with any man, never mind a long distance one. Since she couldn't seem to hold on to a man who was almost living with her, she didn't have much confidence in keeping the attention of one across the country.

Strike three against him was that she was pretty sure he was much younger than she was. She really didn't need to get involved with a twenty-something. A man that age couldn't know what he wanted. He'd end up leaving her for the next woman that piqued his interest.

And that made three strikes against him. But baseball analogy aside, none of that mattered because no phone numbers had been exchanged.

That right there clinched that nothing would ever come of the brief encounter.

Mary Smith, even Mary Elizabeth Smith, was so common a name he wouldn't be able to find her even if he did choose to look her up.

That was good. There was no way for her to talk to him again, even if she had wanted to. Which she didn't.

Or did she?

The doubt in her own mind threw her. So did the shadow of sadness that there was no hope of ever running across him again.

What the hell was that about? Mary Elizabeth mentally slapped herself.

Her psyche and her heart were still too bruised. She didn't trust herself to think straight. She didn't trust her feelings or her instincts anymore. She definitely couldn't trust any imagined interest she might have for him.

In any event, Amanda and Jenny were not going to get off her back about breaking her dry spell with a one night stand if Mary Elizabeth told them the truth—that she'd said goodbye and drove away. And she didn't have it in her to lie to them and make up details about something that didn't happen.

So her only option was to play coy and hope eventually they'd let the damn subject drop.

That was wishful thinking on her part. Her friends could be like dogs with a bone when the subject was juicy enough to whet their appetite. And that kiss they'd witnessed certainly had done that. For Mary Elizabeth too.

Damn it.

She yanked her mind off the memory of the kiss and back to the phone conversation with Amanda. "Anyway, I have to go. I have a meeting in five minutes with the department chair."

Amanda let out a sigh. "Fine, but this conversation isn't over."

"I have no doubt. Bye, Amanda." Mary Elizabeth disconnected the call and tossed the cell into her bag.

It hadn't been a lie. She really did have to run. She was usually fifteen minutes early for everything. If she wasn't early, she felt like she was late, but today Amanda's call had distracted her.

Since it was a Monday morning when many people—students and professors alike—were struggling to get back into work mode after the weekend off, perhaps being on time rather than early would be good enough.

Even so, Mary Elizabeth didn't dally. She moved across the office and through the doorway, locking her office door behind her.

Her department chair's office was on the same floor, but a little ways down the hall.

She covered the distance fast considering her legs were on the short side. A lifetime of walking quickly to keep up with taller people had trained her well and she reached her boss's door in no time.

Knocking she waited until she heard his response before she pushed the door open.

"Mary Elizabeth, on time as always." Donald Brown smiled and waved her inside. "Come in. Please. Sit down."

The man was old as dirt, but he fit the image of

an Art History department chair perfectly, right down to his deeply wrinkled, leathery face beneath the closely cropped graying beard and bushy brows. Donald Brown was the real life personification of many of the historic portraits the students studied.

"Thank you." She moved inside and sank into one of two aging leather office chairs, so fitting with the appearance of the owner of the office himself. "So, to what do I owe the pleasure?"

It wasn't unusual for her and Don to meet to talk. What was unusual was that he had been so elusive as to the meeting's purpose when he'd scheduled it.

His eyes behind his glasses hit upon the open door. Not answering her question he stood and moved across the room to close it.

A closed door meeting? That couldn't be good.

Holy cow. Was she about to be fired? Her heart thundered and her mind raced with scenarios for the reason behind the meeting and the closed door, each worse than the last.

Swallowing hard, she waited as Donald moved back behind the desk and sat.

Leaning forward he said, "Last week I received an odd request."

"Oh?" The word came out sounding calmer than she felt.

"A request for an expert in ancient antiquities. Specifically those from the Middle East."

"Okay." That didn't sound all that strange to her. Nor did it sound like a reason for him to scare her by being so secretive and shutting the door. "I'm not sure that qualifies as odd."

Sure, her concentration of study was probably

less in demand than some others in the field, but there was nothing about it that she thought required a closed door meeting and such hushed tones.

"The request came from the military, actually."

Okay, that was odd. Now she was more intrigued than frightened.

"The military?" she repeated.

He nodded and glanced again behind her.

Frowning, she shot a glance over her shoulder at the door, which remained firmly closed.

She focused back on her boss. "Donald, what going on?"

The older man pressed his lips together and finally said, "Apparently the specific department within the Navy that made the request is responsible for some highly classified stuff. Or at least that's what I gathered from what I could find. I decided to do a bit of research after they did a background check on me before they'd even speak to me. And then, after I recommended you as my choice of top experts in the field in which they were inquiring, they ran a check on you."

"Me?" her voice squeaked.

Don lifted one graying brow. "You are my most qualified expert."

"Thank you, but I'm not sure I want to be now." Not if secretive military agencies with unknown agendas were going to run background checks on her.

He smiled. "I don't think you'll be in any danger. They're not asking you to fly to a warzone. They said they want to meet with you at a facility in Nevada."

A facility?

His words didn't soothe her.

Instead they conjured visions of military facilities shielded by razor wire fences and shrouded in rumors and secrecy.

Places like Area 51. Places that people went into and didn't emerge from. At least not in the same condition as they'd gone in.

She drew in a shaky breath and raised her gaze to her boss. "When would I have to travel to this place?"

Hopefully she'd have time to do some research of her own, or to get more information from the department who'd requested her.

"Tomorrow."

Or maybe she wouldn't have time . . .

CHAPTER SEVEN

The meeting room at NAS Fallon was a lot like every other one Craig had been in during his few years in the teams. Table. Chairs. Whiteboard. Projector. Screen.

The two units training for Navy SEAL Combat Search and Rescue had had their weekend liberty in Sin City, but as of Monday morning it had been back to work, full steam ahead.

Their one reprieve from training had been today for this mysterious lecture.

Craig wasn't complaining. He didn't hate the lectures and seminars they had to sit through. Not like the other guys did.

In his opinion, any event that changed things up a bit was welcome. Besides breaking up the monotony, he usually learned something new and interesting when they had a guest lecturer.

As the older guys grumbled in their seats

surrounding him, Craig kept his optimism and speculation about what they might be here for to himself.

Brody Cassidy leaned closer. "So I spoke to my brother. He's real interested in talking more with us about the Adventure Range setup. You in when we get back to Virginia? We'll probably end up just meeting up at his house."

Chris Cassidy had just gotten married to the sister of a former teammate. From what Craig knew, the Cassidy brothers—southern to the bone—enjoyed good food and drink. Chris's new wife's lasagna was legendary among the guys on the team who'd had the pleasure of eating it so meeting at their house to talk about the shooting range would not be a hardship.

Craig nodded. "Sure. Sounds good. I'm in."

"A'ight. I'll tell him. Thanks."

"No problem." Craig would have met with Brody's brother anyway, but the possibility of a home cooked meal to break up his fast food take out and chow hall existence in the bachelor barracks back on base was extra enticing.

Tompkins, seated on Craig's other side, leaned forward. "Anyone know what this thing is about?"

"Not me." Craig shook his head.

"Nope." Brody snorted. "Waste of time, most like."

Further down the table, Fitz let out a humph of agreement. "Isn't it always?"

"Maybe it's about some new assignment," Craig suggested.

"Doubtful." Brody scowled. "This thing was on

the training schedule command put out last week. Since when are our ops able to be scheduled weeks in advance?"

Fitz snorted. "Not a whole hell of a lot. It's gotta be some bullshit safety lecture or something equally stupid."

Craig remained silent, firmly keeping his own less dim opinion of the proceedings to himself as he waited for the commander to tell them for sure why they were there.

Whatever the reason, it was better than being outdoors working out in full gear in the cold rain.

Of course Craig wouldn't dare bitch about the weather—at least not out loud within hearing of his teammates. But privately, he could be grateful for small things such as today's reprieve from the shitty ice cold rain they were experiencing in the higher elevations in North-West Nevada.

Hopefully they'd get started soon, because sitting around listening to the guys complain was starting to bore him.

Grabbing his cell off the table, he hit the button to see what time it was.

"Well, well, well, things are looking up." Tompkins' comment yanked Craig's attention off his phone.

Craig opened his mouth to ask what was going on, but the words never came out. He could see that clearly for himself.

Besides, after seeing the one woman he'd never expected to encounter again—and at the air station during a team lecture, no less—he wasn't sure he had words to speak anyway.

Mary Elizabeth Smith had entered the meeting room in such deep conversation with his team leader she didn't notice Craig or the room full of men gawking at her.

They all saw her though, which, given what had happened at the bar, could present a problem.

"Oh, hell yeah." Fitz grinned. "A female speaker with a nice rack is always a nice distraction during these bullshit lectures."

"Hey, she kind of looks familiar. Has she spoken to us before?" Tompkins asked no one in particular.

Brody shook his head. "I don't think I've ever seen her before, but that doesn't mean she hasn't talked to you guys and not us."

Listening to the conversation happening over him, Craig swallowed hard and kept his mouth shut. Brody didn't recognize Mary Elizabeth because he had been enjoying his sixty-dollar steak at the Palms in Vegas with Grant Milton and Rocky.

Brody hadn't been out with Craig that night but Tompkins, Fitz and Clyde had been. And they'd seen him leave with the woman about to lecture them.

"I don't know. I think I'd remember if I'd been in a room with her before. Don't you think?" Fitz asked.

Tomkins shrugged. "Yeah, I guess."

Craig held his breath as the guys he'd been with at the bar discussed Mary Elizabeth.

So far, they didn't recognize her. That was a good thing considering the lie they'd both perpetrated on their friends by pretending to hook up.

Who the hell would have ever thought that days later and a five-hour drive from the scene of the crime, that little deception would come back and slap them both in the face?

What happens in Vegas, stays in Vegas. Ha! That catchy marketing phrase was pure bullshit.

He'd never considered how much until right now. But the more he thought about it, the more Craig realized there was plenty of shit that could follow a person home from Vegas. All of it bad.

Quickie weddings. STDs. Unplanned pregnancies. Arrest records. Gambling debt . . .

And in his case, his fake hook up talking to his commander and about to address two units of SEALs he'd have to work with for the foreseeable future.

He couldn't tell them the truth—that he'd lied about going back to his hotel room for some crazy sex with her. He'd never hear the end of it if he admitted that.

But it was so much worse to let them believe she was that kind of woman.

Craig hadn't gone into specifics regarding the supposed wild night, but it seemed the more vague he tried to be, the more elusive with any details, the more the guys assumed. And they had some pretty vivid imaginations when it came to sex of the Vegas one-night stand variety.

His only hope was that Tompkins wouldn't be able to figure out who she was and why she seemed familiar to him.

She was in the same sort of scholarly outfit she'd been wearing that night, but working in his favor was the fact she had her hair up. It was pulled back tightly into a bun, the opposite of that night when it had been down and tumbling temptingly onto her shoulders.

The change in hairstyles altered her looks enough to confuse the other guys, but not him. Not when he'd stared into her eyes—before he'd had his mouth on hers.

Damn. The memory that hit him was still powerful.

Busy with training, he'd been able to push the memories of that night away. It had seemed pointless to relive something that would never happen again.

But now—now he let himself plunge back into the visceral recollection of that night. The sensation of his tongue against hers, of his hands on her body, was still fresh and strong.

Grant Milton, the team leader, cleared his throat and the room quieted down. "I'd like you all to welcome Professor Smith from the Art History department at UNLV."

A professor. Craig smiled at that. The profession suited her perfectly. But he completely understood the frowns and hushed mumbles from the men filling the room.

Why did the team need to know about art history?

"I expect you to give her your undivided attention," Grant continued in a slightly louder tone that immediately silenced the side discussions. "You're going to need the information she's got to share. Somebody hit the lights."

The lights went off. As far as Craig could tell the room went dark before she saw him.

In the dimness of the room lit only by the projector Mary Elizabeth wouldn't be able to see or recognize him so he had a reprieve.

God only knew how she'd react when she did notice him seated there. No doubt she'd be as shocked as he was.

He forced himself to relax and pay attention to the image on her screen until the time of reckoning came.

"The city of Palmyra in Syria," she began and the purpose of this lecture began to become apparent to him and probably to the rest of the men in the room.

The president had just approved the addition of two hundred more troops to be sent to Syria to join the three hundred—mostly special operations forces—already there.

Syria continued to be a hot zone—a three-pronged war between the regime, the rebels and the Islamic State, with Russia and the US involved in various levels, along with the rest of the world as the conflict's impact on the civilians continued to be a worldwide humanitarian crisis.

Craig had assumed the next big battle against ISIS after Mosul in Iraq would be for control of Raqqa so he wasn't surprised they were being briefed about the region. Though he had yet to figure out why the briefing was being conducted by an art history professor.

Mary Elizabeth continued, "The cultural and monetary value of the city's ancient architecture and artifacts of historical significance cannot be denied. However, in 2012 there were reports of various forms of damage and theft. During the years of civil war that followed, the city has been looted by both rebel forces and the regime, and in 2015 by the Islamic State.

"Efforts were made to preserve what could be saved once it became evident the threat of occupation was imminent. As the ISIS forces were growing nearer to Palmyra curators relocated some of the most valuable artifacts to Damascus. When ISIS took control of Palmyra they captured its retired antiquities chief. Khaled al-Asaad was beheaded after refusing to disclose the location of the hidden artifacts.

"Destruction of the historic site's integrity continued unchecked until March of 2016 when the Syrian government, aided by Russian airstrikes, took back control of the city. Unfortunately, in December of 2016 ISIS returned to the city of Palmyra putting the ancient archeological site in jeopardy once again."

She flipped slowly through the images projected on the white wall screen as she spoke. Each photo showed greater devastation than the last.

"The destruction of much of the city's most important sites raises worldwide concern and discussion regarding antiquities in war zones in general. Not just damage and destruction, but also the criminal trafficking of the ancient artifacts. They've even been given a name—*conflict antiquities*—ancient artifacts that are looted, smuggled or sold to fund military or paramilitary activity. Kind of an art for arms exchange, plus anything else the fighters might need.

"But possibly more disturbing is the existence of something that is often denied but that is very real. That is *theft to order*. It's exactly what it sounds like. Middle Eastern antiquities stolen to fulfill specific orders from collectors and dealers willing to pay well. In some cases it's all hushed transactions behind closed doors. In others, it's ridiculously public. Facebook recently shut down a page selling Syrian antiquities.

"And—here's the real punch in the gut—the largest markets are in the US and the UK. It's the law of supply and demand at work. If no one was buying, no one would be looting."

She turned sideways so she could both look at the screen and address the group. It gave Craig the opportunity to observe her more closely.

Mary Elizabeth flipped to other images, speaking passionately about the subject as she did.

Her dedication to her job and to the preservation of history was apparent and admirable. He could hear her emotion about the topic. It was a side of her Craig hadn't seen at the bar. He liked it.

She continued, "Palmyra remains a hotbed of conflict. Russia has embraced the recovery and rebuilding of the city as a kind of pet project, shall we say. They're insisting only they have the knowledge and desire to accomplish what needs to be done there based upon their own experience restoring St. Petersburg. Russia has expressed that their team from the Russian State Hermitage Museum is primed to spearhead the efforts, if the funding comes from the international community, all while being critical of coalition forces—the UK in particular—for not being more vocal about the liberation and future of Palmyra."

CHAPTER EIGHT

"Sadly, destruction, looting and trafficking of antiquities continues around the globe." Mary Elizabeth turned to fully face the room. "If someone could hit the lights, please."

She switched off the projector and, by all evidence, was wrapping up the lecture.

Craig held his breath waiting for her to notice him as the lights came on and she glanced around the room.

"Are there any questions?" she asked.

Tompkins leaned close to Craig and said, "I've got a question. What's she doing tonight and can I be part of it?"

"Shh. You're gonna get us in trouble." Craig shushed Tompkins before Mary Elizabeth heard them.

Tompkins raised one brow. "Sorry. Wouldn't want to get in trouble with the teacher and get detention."

Fitz let out a snort. "I wouldn't mind detention with her."

All the guys in Craig's unit were married or in serious relationships so they tended to not be quite so vocal when it came to females, unlike the guys on the other unit here with them.

Perhaps he was being oversensitive because this woman was not some anonymous female.

In some ways, a very small way, he felt this one was kind of his responsibility. It had his protective streak kicking in. A guy couldn't have a younger sister and not have those instincts.

What compounded it was the fact he'd had his hands and his mouth on Mary Elizabeth. But more so, she had also been on his mind since.

Brody leaned forward. "I've got a question for the lieutenant. What's the stolen artifact trade got to do with us specifically?" he asked loudly enough for his question to reach the front of the room.

Reeling in his attention back to the meeting and off memories of Mary Elizabeth in the casino, Craig remembered she'd asked for questions and Brody's was a good one.

Grant Milton took one step forward. "We're going to table that discussion for now. I'll cover it later with the team. Anything else before I let Professor Smith go?"

Let her go?

Craig's pulse quickened. She must have only been brought in as an expert to speak to them about this one topic.

Once she left this room, he might never see her

again.

Something in him wouldn't let her walk out that door without her knowing he was there. That he'd recognized her—remembered her—even if she had yet to notice him.

He raised his hand. "Sir?"

Fitz let out a chuckle and whispered, "You don't have to raise your hand, kid. We're not in school."

Craig ignored him, instead scrambling for something to ask that wouldn't make him look foolish.

"Dawson." Grant tipped his head toward Craig. "Go ahead."

She noticed him the moment his team leader addressed him. He could tell by the widening of her eyes as the recognition became clear in her expression.

"Um, what percentage, if any, of these artifacts get recovered?" It was a bullshit question, but he'd had to say something.

Under the scrutiny of her gaze, he'd had to reach for anything at all relevant that she hadn't already covered.

She paused for long enough that Grant turned toward her. "Professor Smith?"

"Um, yes. Good question."

She visibly pulled herself together. The others might not have noticed her yanking her professor persona back into place, but Craig sure did.

"The Smithsonian Institute website estimates that approximately half of the fifteen thousand items removed in 2003 from the Iraq Museum in Bagdad have been secured. But as for more recent looting, such as what we're seeing in Syria, the recovery is far less. Aside from the largest architectural elements and sculptures lost forever—irreparably damaged by the Islamic State in a show for the cameras—the number of artifacts being looted for sale that are recovered is very low."

She drew in a breath and visibly slipped further into lecture mode.

"Which is why it's crucial to prevent any future looting. The United Nations Security Council has outlawed trade of the artifacts. But that doesn't help the illegal markets. The fact the FBI has made it publicly known that anyone found buying or selling these artifacts could be prosecuted for aiding terrorism has helped to cool demand.

"The media's coverage and exposure of the problem has been instrumental in helping curb open trade. Curators, dealers, and auction houses are taking note of and reporting questionable items brought to them for sale. There have been calls for special training of customs agents so they'll recognize any items passing through.

"Smaller items are still showing up but the number of larger items has shrunken. However, there are those who know enough to hold on to the most valuable items and wait for five, even ten years until the attention is off them before attempting a sale.

"There have been small victories. A police raid in Bulgaria uncovered a cache of antiquities stolen from a city in Iraq. The US returned sixty-five pieces to the Iraqi government they discovered when a dealer in Dubai tried to sell them to

American museums and galleries using fake documentation. In addition, a US-led raid on an ISIS compound in eastern Syria unearthed an array of artifacts.

"But I do think it's important to note it's not just terrorists, not just the Islamic State, doing the looting. There is satellite evidence, purely circumstantial mind you, that the Syrian government could have profited from massive looting on land which was under their control at the time."

The whole time she'd spoken, she hadn't made eye contact with Craig. Now, as she went silent, she glanced over and finally met his gaze.

Heart pounding, he nodded. "Thank you."

"You're very welcome." She tore her gaze away and glanced at his commander.

As Grant asked for further questions, Tompkins leaned close.

"Kiss ass," he hissed low to Craig.

"Hot for teacher more like." Fitz smiled.

As Craig prayed she didn't hear any of the comments, he waited. The guys would never let him live it down if he rushed up to talk to her just like the school boy with a crush on his teacher that they'd accused him of being.

No more questions came, so Grant nodded. "All right then. Thank you, professor."

"My pleasure." As her gaze cut to Craig one more time, he started to not care what the other guys thought or said.

The need to talk to her before she disappeared strengthened, weighing on him.

He held steady silently willing the commander to call for a break. If only he could go up and say hello to her before she left and . . . and then what?

Get her phone number? Ask her out? He scowled at himself, remembering his life was on a base in Virginia—when he wasn't sent somewhere else in the world. And she, by all indications, lived in Nevada and worked at UNLV.

Craig had always been of the mindset that a person should go all out so he'd never have to look back and wonder *what if?* He hated having regrets.

He feared not doing everything in his power to take her out and get to know her better—a lot better—was about to become one of his biggest regrets.

She was shaking the commander's hand, inching her way closer to the door. Nearer to walking out of his life before he even had a chance with her.

To hell with it.

Craig stood. Ignoring the frowns by the still seated guys around him, he made his way to the front of the room.

"Excuse me, sir. I just wanted to say hello to Professor Smith." He saw Grant raise a brow as he leveled a stare on Craig, prompting him to add, "We've actually met before."

"Oh, really?" Grant's gaze moved to Mary Elizabeth.

Her cheeks flushed as she said, "Yes, actually, we did. Last weekend."

Grant's focus moved back to Craig. "While we were in Vegas on liberty?"

"Yes, sir."

"Um, it's a pleasure seeing you again, Craig. Unexpected . . ." She let the sentence trail off but that one word mirrored how he felt at the surprise reunion.

"Yeah. I know." He let out a short laugh, wishing they were alone for this stilted conversation, or at least not in a room filled with his teammates and his commander.

Still observing them too closely for Craig's liking, Grant widened his stance and folded his arms, one indication he wasn't going anywhere anytime soon.

"Dawson. You go to college?"

"Two years, sir. Back home in New York before I joined up. Got my associates degree." He felt ridiculous saying it.

Mary Elizabeth probably had a masters degree. Or a doctorate or something like that. She wasn't going to be impressed with his two years in college.

Grant turned back to Mary Elizabeth. "Think the kid could pass as one of your students? Or an intern or teacher's assistant, perhaps?"

Her eyes widened. Truth be told, so did Craig's. Mary Elizabeth shook her head, looking as confused as he was. "Um, I—sure. I guess."

Craig moved his attention from her flustered answer to his commander. "Sir?"

"You'll see soon, Dawson. You might want to start brushing up on Middle Eastern antiquities."

Brushing up, as the commander suggested, would require Craig to have had some prior knowledge of the subject, which he certainly did not. He'd majored in political science, not art history. But more important was what else Grant had said. Pass as Mary Elizabeth's student or intern?

What was that about?

"Stop frowning and sit down, Dawson. You'll know soon enough."

"Yes, sir." Reluctantly, Craig nodded a farewell to Mary Elizabeth and went back to his place as ordered.

As Craig retook his seat, he saw Grant ushering her out of the room. She shot him a backward glance before the commander closed the door firmly behind them both.

"What was that about?" Brody asked once Grant was on the other side of the closed door.

Craig blew out a breath. "I wish I knew."

"Holy shit! I just figured out why she looks so damn familiar. You can't see who she is?" Tompkins smacked Fitz and then turned in his chair to face Craig.

Frowning, Fitz asked, "No. Who is she?"

"Why don't you have Dawson tell you? Oh, never mind. I'll tell you. It's too good to let him do it." Tomkins turned to fully face Fitz and Clyde next to him. "She's the woman from the bar in Vegas. The one he left with. Professor Smith is Dawson's dare for a dime."

Fitz widened his eyes. "Well, I'll be damned."

Clyde nodded. "Now that you say it, yeah. I think you're right."

"Yup, I know I am, judging by how pale Dawson just got. I guess that saying is wrong. Huh, Dawson? What happens in Vegas doesn't always stay in Vegas." As Tompkins grinned wide Craig stifled a groan.

Whatever it was that he and the men in this room were going to have to do for the commander's yet undisclosed assignment, it had just gotten a whole lot more complicated.

The only good thing that had happened was that the guys from Craig's own unit had missed the whole conversation about him and Mary Elizabeth in Vegas. They were embroiled in a deep discussion among themselves, trying to guess the nature of their upcoming op while they all waited for the commander to return and explain things.

"Russia." Brody said the single word as if it were self-explanatory.

"Russia?" Rocky repeated.

Brody nodded. "That's got to be what this is all about. Command doesn't need us to deal with whoever is pedaling some stolen old stone shit. This is all about us being close enough to keep an eye on Russia's next move."

"You might be right," Rocky agreed.

"It does make sense." Thom leaned in from farther down the table and joined the discussion. "Think about it. Why wouldn't Russia use rebuilding Palmyra and the like as a good excuse to move freely throughout Syria? They're already in bed with al-Assad. Russia's doing the regime's dirty work for them with their air strikes."

Brody tipped his head in agreement. "So now Russia can have spies on the ground in the guise of antiquities experts. And not just in Syria. Anywhere in the world there are ancient sites. Iraq. Turkey.

Israel."

"But we'll counter that by sending in our own expert," Thom said.

Rocky nodded. "Professor Smith. Backed up by all of us."

Craig had watched the discussion in silence until he could no longer contain the question uppermost in his mind. "But I don't see why the lieutenant would single out me specifically if we're all going to be there."

"Why? What did he say to you?" Rocky asked.

"He asked Mar—" Craig stopped himself before he used her first name. "—the professor if she thought I could pass as her intern."

"Probably because you're the only one of us who can pass for a student."

Craig frowned at Brody. "I'm not that much younger than you."

"Okay. Whatever you say." Brody, in his thirties, scoffed.

There were plenty of guys Craig's age in the teams. He just happened to be on a unit that contained none of them. Some days he was grateful for the years of experience the other guys brought to the table.

Other days—like today—not so much.

"Your age doesn't matter as much as the fact you've got a baby face," Thom said. "If you're clean shaven you can easily look like a college student."

Craig scowled at the baby face comment, but he didn't have time to respond. The door opened and his commander came through again accompanied by Tompkins' team leader.

Facing the room, Grant widened his stance and folded his arms. "Listen up. We've got a lot to cover. Something's just come down from CENTCOM and we're the lucky bastards who got selected for it."

The other team leader stepped forward and dropped a file folder onto the podium. "We'll be joining the special operations forces already on the ground in support of Operation Inherent Resolve."

"But after today's presentation I don't think you'll be surprised to hear that our actual goal will be keeping eyes on any movements made by the Russians on the ground in the region," Grant added.

Brody snorted softly. "Told you so."

Craig shook his head. They'd never hear the end of it now that Brody had guessed right. More importantly, if Brody was correct in his guess that the antiquities recovery would be the cover for their presence it would mean working directly with Mary Elizabeth in some capacity.

Different scenarios spun through his brain as the leaders in the front of the room put new images up on the screen.

Mary Elizabeth could remain in the States and feed them information about the artifacts while he pretended to be her intern and an antiquities expert in the Middle East. That could mean continued, possibly daily contact with her.

He could handle that.

Craig smiled. This might be his best op yet.

CHAPTER NINE

Antsy in her chair in the waiting room, Mary Elizabeth checked the time on her cell phone. She'd been kept cooling her heels, waiting for someone to come and get her for a meeting, for close to an hour.

She had been confused enough when her department chair had told her she'd be lecturing a group of sailors about stolen Middle Eastern antiquities and that her visit here required a background check.

But now she was completely thrown.

First there was the shock of finding Craig, the very hot young guy she'd pretended to pick up last weekend, here too. That had rendered her nearly speechless.

More baffling was when the guy who was apparently in charge had asked her if Craig could pass for an intern. What had that question been about?

And now she was being detained. There was no other way to describe the fact they'd sat her in a room and told her to wait there.

Naval Air Station Fallon was proving to be the scary place she feared it might be.

Her life as a professor was usually uneventful. The biggest excitement being a conference she got to attend, or a new discovery she read about on the internet.

How had she—a boring art history professor—gotten herself involved with the military?

Luckily her boss knew she was here. If for some reason she disappeared, he'd contact someone to look for her.

Now she was just being paranoid.

Though, judging by the really big guns the guards were carrying when she drove through the gate, she wasn't so sure.

She checked the time on her phone again even though only a couple of minutes had passed since the last time.

But this time when she glanced at the screen she noticed something—there was no cell signal, zero, as evidenced by the NO SIGNAL displayed where her signal bars should be.

That was not at all reassuring.

Ready to climb the wall, she stood. A few hesitant steps brought her to the desk. "Um, hi."

The very serious looking man in the blue camouflage uniform sitting behind the desk looked up from his computer screen. "Yes, ma'am."

"Do you know how much longer it will be?"

"I'll be sure to let you know when they're ready

for you, ma'am."

All righty. Not exactly an answer but she felt so far out of her comfort zone here, she didn't have it in her to prod further. "Thanks."

She turned back to the chair again, not sure she could stand to sit still, but figuring this guy would not appreciate if she started pacing.

More time passed—though because of the agitation of the wait making her crazy she couldn't have answered how much time without looking at her cell again. All Mary Elizabeth knew was that it felt like forever.

The door swinging open drew her attention. Her gaze shot from the crack between the tiles she'd been studying, to the man standing in the doorway.

It wasn't the mysterious commander she had been waiting so long to see, but who it was had her jumping up from her seat. "Oh, good. Do you know what's going on?"

Craig took a step back at her attack. "It's a pleasure seeing you again too."

His smile told her he was teasing her, though now was really not the time for jokes.

Still, she apologized. "I'm sorry. I'm just—he told me I couldn't leave. I've been waiting here forever."

He moved to the chair next to the one she'd been sitting in and lowered his big frame into the seat. "Sit."

She did, though she only perched on the edge of the chair.

"You're not used to dealing with the military, are you?" he asked.

"No."

"If there is one thing I've learned since I've been in, it's that you need to get used to waiting. The lieutenant will be here when he gets here."

Mary Elizabeth drew in a breath and let it out slowly. "I'd think the military would be more efficient with their time."

His snort of a laugh forced a small smile from her.

"No?" she asked.

"No." He shook his head.

His joking—but more his reassuring presence—helped her relax enough she didn't feel like bolting out the door and making an escape anymore. But it didn't quell her curiosity.

"Why are you here?" she asked.

Craig lifted one shoulder. "They told me to be here."

"So you really don't know what's going on? Or why I'm here?"

"Those are two different questions."

She narrowed her eyes at him. "You know something."

He dipped his head. "I do. We had a briefing with the team."

"So why—"

Craig held up his had and stopped her mid-sentence. "I don't know the details about your involvement. Or why I've been called here either, for that matter. The briefing was very general . . . and classified."

She let out a *humph* she couldn't control.

That only had him smiling. "Sorry. I'm sure

CAT JOHNSON

we'll know soon enough."

"Fine." She had a feeling she was scowling as she said it.

He continued to smile. "It really is good to see you again. It's pretty crazy, you know, since I never got your phone number the other night."

They had an agreement to get their respective friends off their mutual backs. Nothing more. Why would he want her phone number?

Unless he was interested in her. Maybe there was more than just a mutually beneficial arrangement for him between them.

He was handsome and sweet and he kissed really, really well but it didn't matter. The idea of getting involved with any man in any way other than as coworkers or casual acquaintances held no appeal for her.

She must really be as broken as she feared she was, because he really was a good guy.

And, admittedly, pretty damn hot.

Even if she didn't trust her instincts when it came to the male sex any longer, her friends certainly thought highly of what they'd seen of him. She'd been dodging the conversation with them about him since that night.

Her friends had once accused her of being a block of ice on the inside. Sitting next to Craig now and feeling not even a twinge of interest, Mary Elizabeth was starting to wonder if her friends were right.

But then there was that kiss.

She'd felt something during that.

Circumstances. Nothing more. Of course she'd

gotten caught up in the moment at the bar. The glow of lights. The abandonment of her inhibitions brought on by the drinks. The excitement of the lie. His lips on her as his hands tangled in her hair . . .

She cleared her throat and yanked her traitorous mind off the memory that might start to melt her long frozen center.

"So, you're a sailor?" she asked.

"Yup." He dipped his head. "And you're a professor."

"I am."

"I guess we didn't have a lot of time to exchange small talk the other night, did we?"

Before he'd planted the lip lock she couldn't shake the memory of on her and then they'd parted ways? "No, we didn't."

"So maybe we should," he said. "Talk. Get to know each other."

She had a strong feeling he meant on a date. She didn't want to hurt his feelings. It was far easier to play dumb, so she said, "Sure. It seems we have plenty of time now so I'll start. Do you live here on the base?"

"No, I don't. We're only here at the air station for training."

Base. Air station. She wasn't even sure of the difference. His short simple answer had shown her exactly how little she knew about the military—and consequently this man as well.

Choosing to not comment on her own ignorance since he hadn't, she asked, "You're here from where?"

"The east coast."

He wasn't very forthcoming with his answers.

Never one to be able to resist a challenge, she found that his elusiveness only raised her interest.

She was just determining which course of questioning to take to get some answers out of him when he leaned forward, bracing his forearms on his knees, and said, "So, um, you know our little charade the other night?"

"For our friends, you mean?"

"Yup." He nodded. "There might be a problem."

She'd already realized their show had ended up causing as many problems as it had solved since her friends were relentless in their questioning as they pressed her for details.

What happened? Are you going to see him again? Why not? Why didn't you get his number? Why, why, why—it was enough to drive her crazy. But she wasn't sure why he was having problems. Were men as relentless in their prying into each other's love lives as women?

"What do you mean?" she asked. "My friends bought it completely. They're prodding me for information about you."

"Mine were too, about you. That's what I mean. It might have worked a little too well. They believe we spent the night together." He'd lowered his voice to a mere whisper to deliver that last sentence.

He really was a cute guy. She smiled. "It's okay. That's fine. It's not like I'm going to ever see—" The possible problem hit Mary Elizabeth as her brain connected the dots. She resigned herself to his answer as she asked, "Your friends are here, aren't they?"

"Yeah. The two guys I was with at the bar are here with me for training." A pained expression crossed his face. "And they were in your lecture. And they recognized you."

"Oh."

"I didn't tell them anything at all. I swear to you, but even so, they still think you and I left the bar together. And they saw that kiss so . . ." He pressed his lips together. "I'm sorry."

"No. It's my own fault. It was all my idea."

Of course, at the time she had come up with the idea, she hadn't known she'd be summoned to an Naval air station or that Craig and his buddies were in the Navy, but hindsight was twenty-twenty.

So they were here and they'd recognized her. It wasn't the ideal situation—it definitely made her uncomfortable—but she could live with knowing two men in her lecture assumed she'd picked up Craig for a one-night stand at a bar in Vegas.

It wasn't as if Craig's friends were students she'd have to face all semester. Her being here today was a one time thing. She'd never see these guys again.

There was a brief moment of regret that she also wouldn't see this very nice guy she'd shared a plan and a kiss with again after today either, but she forced that thought away. All she had to do is think about the last guy she'd invited into her life.

Her cold dead heart was a good reminder to not do the same again soon, if ever. Especially with a man who lived thousands of miles away. And was too young. And was in the Navy traveling who knew where and for how long.

Still, it had been nice having Craig as a partner in crime, even if his friends did assume all sorts of things about her now.

As Craig continued to look miserable—she could only assume with his guilt over ruining her reputation—she smiled. "It's okay. Really. My life is so boring, having the guys you were with think I'm a bad girl is a nice change."

It was kind of fun, actually. Her quiet life—not to mention her profession—didn't lend itself to bad girl experiences. Her one night in Vegas was pretty exciting though, even if nothing had happened.

"Still. I apologize. I never even considered you'd end up here. That command would bring you in to speak to the team is—"

"Crazy, I know." She laughed. "It is a pretty insane coincidence. But it really was nice running into you again too."

He drew in a breath and opened his mouth to speak when the door swung open again. Grant Milton—she'd be damned if she could remember what his rank was—popped his head in.

"Dawson. Professor. Team meeting room. Now."

Grant Milton was certainly a man of few words but he didn't seem to need more. Craig was out of the chair and standing in a split second.

Not used to responding to commands, she took a few seconds longer to process the order, grab her bag and get to her feet. By then Craig was already holding the door open, waiting for her to walk through.

"Thank you."

He nodded his response as he closed the door

behind her. Apparently Craig knew where they were supposed to go because he led them down a hallway and to a room.

As Craig stood back to let her enter first, she became very aware of his hand pressed to her lower back. It was brief—only a second as he guided her through the door then it was gone—but the feel of his touch remained.

She realized her heart might be cold and dead, and her brain was firmly shut down to any and all romantic notions, but her body still had the capacity to respond to a hot guy's touch.

Not quite sure how to deal with that reality she decided to push all thoughts of it aside. Facing Grant, seated at a large table in this sparsely decorated room filled with not much more than chairs she had enough to deal with.

"So, professor, we have a proposition for you."

"Who exactly is *we*?" she asked.

He smiled. "You're a question asker, aren't you?"

Mary Elizabeth lifted her brow. "No— " She stopped herself, realizing he was right, and changed direction. "Wouldn't you be if you were in my situation?"

"I would." He nodded. "I, acting on behalf of the United States, have a proposition for you."

She glanced sideways and caught Craig's expression. He seemed amused by the conversation, judging by his half smile.

"This is amusing to you?" she asked.

He had said he was as much in the dark as she was, so why wasn't he more serious about this mysterious proposition?

He sobered immediately. "No, it's not. Sorry."

Now his commander looked entertained. "Remind me again, professor, how it is that you two know each other?"

Uh oh. "Um, we ran into each other in Vegas."

"During our liberty last weekend," Craig added.

"Okay." Grant Milton of the forgotten rank smiled. "Well, it's good that you're familiar with each other since you'll be working together on this."

"And what exactly is *this*?" she asked, realizing she really was a question asker, just like he'd said.

"If you agree, you're going to be joining a team of experts working on recovering and restoring lost Middle Eastern antiquities."

It sounded like a dream job. But also like it would involve a lot of work and time. She had a full course load at the university this semester. "When would I be starting?"

"Immediately."

"But I have classes—"

"Your boss has already approved the leave."

Approved the leave she hadn't even known about until this second? The whole urgency made her feel uncomfortable, as did the fact the decisions seemed to all have been made without her consent.

Now she had a dozen more questions. "Where would I be working *if* I take this job?"

"We'd need you there on site evaluating the objects recovered."

"And on site is where?"

"Iraq mostly. Perhaps Damascus. Maybe Turkey.

Possibly elsewhere, as needed. Russia is a possibility, as well, depending."

Iraq? Syria? Turkey? Russia? Her eyes widened. She glanced at Craig beside her and he appeared as surprised as she was by this new information.

"You'd want her on site, sir?" Craig asked.

He raised a brow. "Yes, Dawson. Problem?"

"No, sir."

Craig might not have a problem with this plan, but she sure did.

"But there's a war on," she said.

The commander smiled. "Yes, I'm aware."

"I'm a civilian."

"I'm also well aware of that." His smile widened.

"Isn't it dangerous over there?"

"You'd be working mostly on US bases and you wouldn't be alone. The men in your lecture today will accompany you."

She didn't want to question the capabilities of the US Navy but this was her life they were talking about. She read enough news reports to think she shouldn't be over there where they were going to send her.

"No offense, but is a roomful of sailors going to be able to protect me in the warzone?"

"No offense taken. They're actually quite capable, as far as sailors go." The commander's lips twitched. "And you'll also be assigned your friend Dawson here to shadow you. He'll be your right-hand man. Your companion twenty-four/seven."

Her companion twenty-four/seven?

That had her swallowing hard.

Her fear of bodily injury or death in the warzone aside, Craig's constant presence was going to be another issue she'd have to wrestle with.

With mixed feelings about that as her body warred with her mind and her heart, she said, "That's *if* I take the assignment."

"You'll take it." Grant looked incredibly confident.

His attitude had her immediately challenging him. "Oh? What makes you so sure?"

"You're passionate about this subject. And you know it's a chance of a lifetime. You can go back to teaching art history to bored students trying to fill an elective in their course schedules, or you can be part of history.

"*And* because State Department research shows that ISIS has an Antiquities Division dedicated to researching known archaeological sites, exploring new ones, organizing the looting and marketing of the stolen antiquities and I think that pisses you off.

"And because if you take this opportunity you know you can help save Palmyra, Mosul, Dura Europos, Apamea and other ancient cities in Iraq and Syria. You can work alongside renowned experts from all over the world. You can save the past that's been lost and rebuild it for future generations."

Grant smiled. "Perhaps I don't know you very well, professor, but I know passion and dedication when I see it. And I don't think you can say no to all that."

Dammit. She hated that Grant was right, but she'd hate even more living with the regret for the rest of her life if she said no and missed this opportunity.

"No. I can't say no to all that." She glanced at Craig—her shadow in the warzone twenty-four/seven—and found him watching her.

She'd figure out a way to resist him.

The feel of his hand on her back returned, followed quickly by the memory of their one kiss.

Or maybe she wouldn't.

CHAPTER TEN

"Thank you, professor. Someone will be in touch very soon with the details," Grant said.

"And until then I can't talk to anyone." Mary Elizabeth didn't look too happy.

In fact, Craig had noticed she hadn't looked happy for the past half hour. Not since his commander had laid out for her the cover story they'd worked out followed by a warning to tell no one she'd be working with the military and the importance of operational—as well as national—security.

That was probably about the time she started to figure out this opportunity was about way more than just saving artifacts and antiquities.

"Oh, you can talk to people all you want, professor. Just not about the specific details of this assignment." The commander smiled, which only had her scowling more deeply.

She was definitely not used to being on the receiving end of commands.

The situation might be amusing if Craig weren't the one who'd be personally responsible for her. And if he didn't have to deal with Tompkins and the other guys and their assumptions and teasing. But he'd made his bed, so to speak, and he'd lie in it.

Too bad Mary Elizabeth wouldn't be in his bed with him to make it all worthwhile.

She stood from her chair and glanced at him before saying to Grant, "I'll wait for my instructions then . . . and brush up on cultural protocols in the meantime."

"Excellent. You're going to do fine."

"And if I don't?" she asked, the challenge clear in her tone.

"There is a plan for that contingency, as well, along with a highly trained team to back it up," Grant said.

"Well, that's comforting." Her gaze moved from the commander to Craig, before she turned to go.

Craig jumped to his feet, intending to ask to be dismissed and follow her out.

"Dawson. Stay."

"Yes, sir." He'd been hoping to walk her to her car. Or at least have a few moments to speak to her given the recent turn of events, to make sure she was okay with it all.

That was obviously not going to happen.

After one more backward glance, Mary Elizabeth closed the door behind her and was gone.

"Please tell me you didn't have sex with her."

The commander's question brought Craig's

attention around. He felt the blood leave his face. "No, sir. I did not."

"Good."

No doubt the commander was relieved. That would have probably messed up the plan.

But there was the other issue of Tompkins. "But—"

"I don't like that word, Dawson. It's usually followed by something I don't want to hear."

"Yes, sir. I apologize."

Grant sighed. "Get on with it. Tell me your *but*."

"It's nothing, sir."

"You sure about that, Dawson?" Grant lifted his brows.

"Yes." Craig would set the other guys straight on his own.

There was no need to involve command in their little bar game.

It would be embarrassing, but he'd do it. Confess the truth to Tompkins and the others and make sure Mary Elizabeth went into this assignment with the clean slate she deserved.

The commander eyed him for an uncomfortably long time. "I hope so. All right. You're dismissed."

"Yes, sir." Craig nodded and turned to go, happy to be getting out from under his commander's scrutiny. Less happy he'd have to go own up to his lie.

They'd all been cut loose for the day after the lecture and following briefing, so Craig headed to the chow hall in hopes of finding the guys. It was late enough he figured they could be eating dinner.

He was right. He found the guys from his own

unit at a table.

He sat and got a sideways glance from Brody. "You not eating?"

"I will." Craig sighed and looked around the dining hall. "You see Tompkins around?"

"Nope." Brody shook his head while tearing into a fried chicken leg.

"You guys have gotten real chummy on this trip," Thom said.

"Not really. We just hung out that one night in Vegas. That's all." The night this mess started.

Thom shrugged. "No need to get defensive. I wasn't making anything of it. Just an observation."

"I know." Craig let out a huff again.

Rocky dropped his fork on his tray and frowned. "All right. Spill it. What's wrong?"

"And does it have anything to do with the hot teacher from today you ran up to talk to?" Thom asked.

"Leave the kid alone. You're making him nervous." Mack snorted. "He looks like he might pass out."

"I'm not nervous." And he sure as hell wasn't going to pass out. More, he was tired of being considered the kid on the team. Craig scowled at the bullshit he should be used to by now. "I've just got a lot on my mind."

"Such as the hot teacher?" Brody laughed, joining in the joke now that his chicken was down to nothing but a bone.

"You should all be a little more concerned about this op too. We're going to be responsible for a civilian in a whole lot of places that she probably would be better off not being."

Brody lifted a shoulder. "It wouldn't be the first time."

"Or the last," Rocky added.

"So the kid's problem is definitely the hot teacher." Thom grinned. When Craig let out a huff and stood, Thom said, "Aw, jeez. Don't walk away mad, Dawson. We're just messing with you."

Scowling, Craig shook his head. "I'm not mad. I'm getting food."

"Yeah, let him eat. He's a growing boy." Rocky grinned.

Deciding they didn't need the encouragement of any response, Craig walked away and joined the line.

His teammates might suck, but at least the air station had decent food. Probably better than they'd get on the upcoming op.

Poor Mary Elizabeth. He'd bet this assignment was going to be her first experience with chow hall food.

As he retook his seat at the team's table, food tray in hand, he wondered how she was going to do . . . and with that thought he realized this woman was already uppermost on his mind and the assignment hadn't even begun yet.

Not good.

"Hey, Dawson. There's Tompkins." Brody lifted his chin toward the entrance.

Craig had been about to take his first bite of hot fried chicken but this was more important. He put the drumstick down and stood.

"Be right back." Pausing, he added, "Leave my

food alone while I'm gone."

Brody's lips twitched. "Sure. No problem."

Craig sighed, assuming he'd at least be missing the piece of cake he'd grabbed for dessert by the time he got back. But this was more important.

He worked his way over to Tompkins. "Hey."

"Hey, lover boy. What's up?" Tompkins asked.

Great. A new nickname. *Lover boy* was possibly worse than *kid*. He had yet to decide.

Craig drew in a bracing breath. "I need to talk to you about Mary Elizabeth.

Tompkins' brows rose high. "Do you call her Mary Elizabeth in bed or Professor Smith? That could make for some interesting roleplaying, I suppose."

"Tompkins. Listen to me. I didn't have sex with her. I didn't even go home with her. I walked her to her car and then went back to my hotel room alone."

"Sure you did. Good try. You get points for trying to protect her, but no go. We all saw you kissing her. Nobody is going to believe you didn't seal the deal."

"But I didn't. It was all for show. She wanted to go home but her friends were pressuring her to stay. You guys had dared me. So she and I made a deal to get you all off our backs by pretending to leave together."

Tompkins shook his head. "Not buying it, Dawson. But don't worry. We're all adults here. It's no big deal that you two did the horizontal mambo."

The man slapped him on his back and was about to head for the food line when Craig laid a hand on his arm to stop him. "It kind of is a big deal. I just met with my lieutenant. She's going overseas with us. She's going to be on the op."

"Really? I'll be damned. Lucky you, huh?" A mischievous grin lit Tompkins' face before he slapped Craig one more time on the back and headed for the chow line.

Craig bit back a curse, seriously hoping command's plans for this op went better than his and Mary Elizabeth's Vegas bar plan had.

CHAPTER ELEVEN

"You're going where?" Drink poised in mid-air, Amanda widened her eyes.

"Tell me you didn't just say the Middle East." Jenny looked equally shocked.

The list of things Mary Elizabeth wasn't allowed to discuss with anyone seemed longer than what she was permitted to talk about. That made telling her friends she was leaving for a job somewhere in the Middle East extra difficult.

"Stop looking at me like that. To be able to work with a team of experts recovering and restoring the ancient sites destroyed by the war is an amazing opportunity."

"But it's the Middle East," Jenny repeated. "And there's a war on."

Amanda nodded in agreement. "Right? It seems like everyone is fighting each other over there."

"The Smithsonian has a team over there too. We have to go where the antiquities are. We have to protect what remains from further damage, as well as try to recover what's been stolen."

"Why do you have to go there? There's the internet. They can send you pictures. You can study them at the university."

"It's not the same. The counterfeit artifact trade is huge. I have to see the pieces for myself. Touch the items. Weigh them. Look at them beneath a scope. Test them for age." All of the reasons were valid but they seemed to not impress her friends at all as they continued to shake their heads and look at her as if she was insane.

Maybe they were right and she was crazy.

Grant Milton had told her to expect to be away for six weeks. Craig had warned her schedules were fluid in the military—which was not an encouraging thought. He told her to assume it would be double that and she should be prepared to be away for three months and then just be pleasantly surprised if it was less.

That conversation had blown her opinion of the Navy as a tightly run ship right out of the water. Bad puns aside, that hadn't helped her nerves.

At this point her life had taken such a turn for the surreal she wasn't sure of much anymore except that the Navy had made plans for her to travel on a date she wasn't allowed to disclose to anyone. A date Craig had warned her would likely change—more than once—so it was better that she couldn't tell anyone when she was leaving anyway.

She had to try one more time to impress upon her friends the enormity of this opportunity. She'd be saving history. She'd be contributing to something lasting. Something for future generations that would survive long after she was gone.

What if one hundred years ago British archaeologist Howard Carter had decided it was too risky to explore Egypt? The world might never have discovered the wonders of King Tut's tomb.

She had the chance to leave her mark on the world and she was going to take it.

Besides, what did she have keeping her here? No boyfriend, *that* was painfully true. She didn't even have a cat. Her one houseplant she'd give to Amanda or Jenny.

"I'll be working with some of the top rated people in my field. People I've only read about. A team from the Hermitage. It's a once in a lifetime opportunity."

"A chance of a lifetime that could cost you your life. There's a war on." Jenny was starting to repeat herself.

"Not just a war. I know you're too cerebral to watch television but you do know what's happening over there, right?" Amanda asked.

"She's right." Jenny nodded. "I seriously hope you're not traveling to Syria. Have you seen that mess?"

Mary Elizabeth frowned. "I know what's happening. I read the news every day."

"Then you should know about ISIS. On top of that there's a civil war in Syria. And you want to go over there? On purpose?" Jenny asked.

"And don't forget about Russia bombing everything. What if you're caught in an airstrike?" Amanda added.

None of this was news to Mary Elizabeth. Her friends concerns mirrored everything she'd thought herself. Yet she was still going.

If she looked deeper into why she was set on going she'd have to admit it was more than simply the reasons she'd already given her friends.

Yes, those were all valid and true, but it was more than that. It was the fact that she'd done everything she was supposed to do in life and all it had done is dump her in a rut she felt she couldn't get out of.

She'd studied hard in school, which had led to her excelling in her field. Yet in her classroom at the university—teaching the same courses and the same things to an ever-changing rotation of students who seemed more the same than different—she felt trapped by an invisible box of her own creation.

Rather than spinning her wheels trying to get out of this self-created rut on her own, she could accept the push that this opportunity offered.

In her personal life she'd never gone out and played the field. Never just been in anything for a good time. She'd gone from one long-term relationship to the next, spanning twelve years and only two serious boyfriends. Yet now she was not only alone and single again, she was twitchy and leery from the devastating end of the last relationship insuring she'd remain alone for a good long time.

Feeling as she did now, no relationship stood a chance of even getting off the ground. In this mindset if she saw a spark of a relationship she'd be inclined to stomp it out before it burnt down her world completely like the last one had.

Given that, why not travel to Iraq and Syria and Turkey and Russia? The thrill of just the thought of the travel—the things she'd get to see and do—sent a zing through her. It aroused an excitement far better than the promise of love.

Her accomplishments, any strides she made at the ancient sites that needed her help so badly, wouldn't come back to bite her like the supposed love of her life and man of her future had.

If flying to Iraq was what she needed to do to break out of her rut, then that's what she was going to do, dammit.

She set her jaw. "Life isn't without risk. Not even my life on campus. That is a fact. So I might as well get out and live—really live."

Amanda made a face. "That's very philosophical of you."

"It's true." The evidence was in the same news reports her friends were quoting to keep her from going.

Shooters. Bombings. Plane crashes. Train derailments. Car accidents. Overturned busses. Terrorists. Lone wolves. Gun-toting drivers with road rage—she could barely keep up with the bad news.

Living alone, commuting to work with the crazy drivers on the roads, and walking alone across campus—none of that was without a certain amount of risk.

Honestly there was a good chance she'd be safer where she was going. There she would be under the care of the roomful of military men she'd been brought in to lecture.

Them and Craig. Twenty-four/seven.

Craig, who was too young. Too nice. Too sweet . . . Too hot. Too good of a kisser. Too tempting to her body that had been too long ignored.

She broke away from that dangerous train of thought.

If forgetting that kiss and resisting him was the biggest worry she had over there while she got to work in her dream job she'd call it a win and walk away happy.

"Can't you just *really live life* with that hottie you left with from the bar the other night?" Amanda's uncanny question about Craig—as if she could tell he was in Mary Elizabeth's thoughts—had her nearly choking on the liquid she'd been about to swallow.

Jenny nodded. "I like that plan. He was a cutie."

Hoping the truth wasn't written all over her face—that she was going to be with Craig for the foreseeable future—Mary Elizabeth tried to get her friends off the subject. "I'm not going to be dependent on a man for my happiness ever again. I need to make my own."

"And this job will do that?" Amanda asked.

"Yes. I really think it will." Unfortunately, a man was going to be her shadow, making her vow to herself a bit more difficult.

Reaching for her drink, Mary Elizabeth took a long swallow and wondered if there would be a bar where she was going.

~ * ~

"Thanks for coming over. I know you guys are

shipping right out again so I appreciate your taking the time." Chris Cassidy popped the tops off two long neck bottles. He walked around the kitchen island and handed one to his brother Brody and the other to Craig.

They were there to give Chris any information they could about The Adventure Range they'd been to in Vegas. Brody had said Chris was kicking around the idea of opening something like it locally.

Craig had no problem talking about their time in Vegas since he'd bested the older guys on the range and won the hundred dollar bet.

They'd all assumed their years of experience would put them over the top so his teammates had no problem each kicking in twenty bucks to go to the winner. They'd never thought Craig would win. They'd assumed his youth would work against him.

What they didn't realize was his dedication to the softer side of being a good sniper. His study and practice of not just the technical aspects but also the finer points—body position, breathing, trigger squeeze, mental management, even diet.

Craig's willingness to admit he didn't know everything, and his dedication to continued and constant learning, as well as his commitment to details had been enough to win him some cash. But more than that, it hopefully gained him a bit of respect.

Even if it hadn't, today was turning out to be good. Seated on the sofa in front of the large screen television on the wall, Craig drew in a long sip and appreciated the cold tasty brew as it slipped down his throat.

He glanced at the label. It was the good stuff. Way better than the cans he grabbed by the six-pack at the commissary and kept in his fridge in the bachelor barracks.

Meanwhile, something was cooking in the kitchen that filled the house with an aroma that had Craig's mouth watering the moment he'd walked through the door.

A night spent with teammates and their family, a home cooked meal and good beer, all in a real home with a deck and a yard. What could be better? He'd even spotted a corn hole game out in the yard. Maybe they'd get to play later.

Compared to his sad lonely room on base, Chris's house felt like Disneyland—the happiest place on earth.

Yeah, it wasn't a real hardship being there. Craig let out a laugh. "Really, Chris. No thanks necessary. Anytime."

"The kid's easily bought with food and booze," Brody said.

"Ain't nothing wrong with that." Chris let out a snort. "And so are you, baby brother. So are you."

Hearing Brody get teased about his age by his older brother—after Brody was always teasing Craig about his age—was just icing on the cake of this night.

Craig laughed. "How's it feel getting ragged on?"

Brody let out a snort. "It feels like my bro is getting old and is just jealous of me."

"Yup. That's it." Chris rolled his eyes at Brody and then turned his attention to Craig. "He giving you a hard time?"

Craig lifted one shoulder. "Eh, he's just getting old and is feeling jealous of me and my youth, I think."

Chris barked out a laugh as Craig turned Brody's words back on him.

Brody cocked a brow at Craig. "Looks to me like Tompkins and the guys from his team give you way more shit than any of us do."

"Yeah." Craig drew in a breath and decided he'd better confide in Brody. Both teams would be heading to Iraq in just days—with Mary Elizabeth. "Actually, I wanted to talk to you about that."

Since the guys from the other team hadn't believed him he needed backup to help protect her from the mess they'd made.

Brody and Chris exchanged glances.

Chris stood. "This sounds like it's going to be serious."

"You don't have to leave," Craig said.

"Oh, I'm not. Just let me get myself a fresh beer first before you start." Chris grinned.

Craig regretted saying anything already. "It's not a big deal."

"What you don't understand, kid, is that Chris's life is so boring since his retirement from the teams, he needs to live vicariously through us."

Shaking his head as he walked, Chris returned to the living room with a bottle for himself. He sat in the chair facing the sofa where Craig sat. "Ignore him and go on."

With the two Cassidy brothers focusing their complete attention on him, Craig rethought the whole thing.

He'd deal with the situation with Mary Elizabeth himself. Maybe Tompkins and the guys would keep their mouths shut about what they thought they knew.

Hell, maybe they'd forget about that whole night once they were over there and it was time for work and not time for play.

And maybe after spending twenty-four/seven shadowing Mary Elizabeth, what the guys thought had happened actually would.

Shit. He couldn't even let himself think that, no matter how much he'd enjoy it.

Time to change the subject before he made everything worse for her.

"It's nothing. Really." Craig turned to Chris. "You have a chance to check out that cell phone video Brody took of us shooting at the range in Vegas?"

CHAPTER TWELVE

"You go nowhere without me." Craig said as they stood in the surreal space that was supposed to be her home for the next six weeks . . . or more.

She was rethinking this trip. But it was a little too late for that. In her tactical pants, boots, and body armor, she felt as far away from her usual life as she was from home.

He continued, "You go nowhere alone. If I'm not with you, one of the other guys will be. This might be a US base and we are in charge of the operations but there could be men from any of the sixty-six countries in the coalition here. I don't want you wandering around alone among them. Okay?"

Mary Elizabeth was smart enough to know he was right. Better safe than sorry. Even so, she wrinkled her nose at being ordered around. "Fine. Though I don't know where you think I'll be going. It's not exactly a vacation resort."

Craig tipped his head to the side. "It's not so bad here. There's a gym tent with Crossfit equipment, the recreation center has Wi-Fi and the food isn't too bad in the chow hall."

She resisted the urge to roll her eyes at his list of amenities.

"All right. Next. Your flak jacket is too be worn at all times."

She felt the weight of the body armor he was so adamant she wear pressing on her shoulders and had to think there'd be no need to work out in a gym after wearing this stuff all day. She used to think her underwire bra was uncomfortable, but compared to this thing, that small discomfort was nothing.

Again, she made a face.

He noticed. "I know. Body armor is hot and heavy and uncomfortable, but it can save your life so you'll have to deal with it. You walk to the shower, you have it on. You go to eat in the chow hall, you have it on. You go to bed at night—"

Seeing the trend, Mary Elizabeth anticipated the order and cut him off by saying, "I have it on."

Craig smiled, breaking the very serious lecture he'd been subjecting her to. "No, you can take it off to sleep but the minute you get up, you put it on."

"Yes, sir." She executed a salute that only had him smiling broader.

Shaking his head, he said, "Don't do that again. Or at least let me teach you how to do it right. Okay?"

"Roger that."

He smiled broader. "Smart ass."

She didn't know where this light and airy joking

side of her came from. It was possibly from the mania bubbling just below the surface inside her caused by her bone deep fear of being in the war zone.

Even with a dozen Navy men, who she was strongly starting to suspect were not just normal sailors, her fear was very real.

She was in a foreign land, under foreign rule. A place where women were second-class citizens at best and Americans were considered a mortal enemy by some.

A region where, in spite of what she'd heard about a withdrawal of US troops, there was obviously a strong military presence. At least that's what she surmised by the number of US military aircraft standing ready on the tarmac when she'd flown in.

Yet here she was—dammit—and for the exact reason Grant Milton had said she'd be here. The once in a lifetime opportunity was too good to pass by.

She glanced at the jacket. It was ugly and heavy and unwieldy and she had to wear it all of her waking hours or risk dying.

Was her passion for her job going to cost her life?

"Let's go over how this fastens so you can get it on and off easily yourself."

The ever present undercurrent of sexual tension between them should have been broken as they moved back into the safe waters of work mode, but it wasn't. Not with him basically showing her how to disrobe from her body armor.

Instead, she was very aware of the intimacy of the action as he helped her take off the vest, then put the vest back on. Showed her how to fasten it, and then how to unfasten it again.

She searched for something to say to break the tension. "It's heavy."

"I know. You'll get used to it." He bobbed his head to one side. "Eventually."

Maybe he had gotten used to it, but she doubted she would.

She must have been frowning or scowling because he pinned her with a gaze and smiled. "You really are going to get to do your job while you're here. I promise. They'll be all sorts of dusty things for you to . . . clean or catalog or whatever you do with them."

She let out a laugh. "Some intern you are."

Shyly adorable, he lifted one shoulder. "I'm willing to learn. If you want to teach me."

That sounded better to her than it should. Being around him all the time, even while wearing the stupid vest and whatever else they subjected her to, was proving to be tempting. Even while in this horrible room—if she could even call it that—that they'd assigned her to.

Her quarters felt more like a shipping container than a bedroom. The complete lack of windows was as comforting as it was disturbing. She couldn't see out, couldn't see what was happening beyond her confines, but she also didn't have to worry about anyone seeing in . . . or bullets flying in.

That last thought gave her pause.

Though according to what little the commander

had told her she could be moving around quite a bit. She'd be working mainly out of the Iraqi Institute for the Conservation of Antiquities and Heritage facility in Erbil, but there was the possibility of an occasional trip to the Iraq Museum in Bagdad.

Being in Erbil was exciting enough to have the historian inside her tingling. The city, with its magnificent Citadel, fountain-adorned garden squares, colorful bustling bazaar and esteemed universities, had the distinction of being the oldest continuingly inhabited city in the world.

Working in this diversely populated ancient city was a dream come true for someone who loved ancient history as much as she did. And it was, but with the history came the reality of the dangers of a modern war, with the city and its population not nearly far enough from the front line of the war against ISIS.

Before she began to panic further about her location and its proximity to some very bad things that were happening, Mary Elizabeth moved the subject back to the specifics of her work and one of many questions she still had.

"What's happening tomorrow morning?"

Tomorrow, leaving base and her first day at the Institute, was on her mind. She'd be able to relax more if she got the question answered.

He lifted a brow. "You mean logistically?"

She nodded.

"Right after we eat here in the chow hall, we'll be traveling to the Institute in non-tactical vehicles—"

"What's that?" she asked.

"Military speak for civilian SUVs," Craig said with a small smile.

"Is that safe?" She'd been picturing more like a tank or at least a Humvee.

"With me in the vehicle with you and four more operators shadowing us in another, yeah, I think it's safe. Erbil's generally a peaceful, safe city."

She eyed Craig's gun and knife. She had no doubt the other men acting as her escort would be armed to the teeth while traveling through the city. Probably more armed than they already were just walking around base.

"Okay. I trust you."

"Good. I'm glad. Anything else you have questions about?"

Only a dozen or so . . .

"Why am I sleeping here on base? Wouldn't it be easier if I were staying at the Institute since I'm working there? I read there are dormitories—"

"Yeah, no. Not gonna happen." He shook his head.

"Why not?" she asked.

"Because we can protect you better here. I'm right next door. In fact, we share a wall." He pointed to the wall behind her bunk bed. "You can just knock and I'll be here in seconds."

Aside from the fact he'd be sleeping mere inches from her, right on the other side of the ugly wall, something else he'd said cut through and scared her.

"You can't protect me at the Institute? But I'm going to be there everyday." Her renewed panic came through in her voice. She heard it in her heightened tone.

"I will—we all will—protect you wherever you are. And in addition to coalition forces there are three hundred and fifty thousand Peshmerga keeping Erbil safe from Daesh, but logistically it's easier to secure you here at night in an installation we control. Call me crazy but I don't blindly trust easily and I don't trust anyone to be able to keep you as secure as my team can and that includes our allies. Okay?"

Mary Elizabeth drew in a breath. "Okay."

She said it but she didn't exactly feel it. She didn't know as much about this region of northern Iraq as she should but she knew enough to assume it wasn't safe. The only question was, how dangerous was it?

"Hey. You all right?" Craig took another step forward, impressing upon her how close they were. How alone as they stood closely together.

This felt different than the short time they'd spent together that night in Vegas. Now they were in her living quarters on a base in Iraq.

Hiding any doubt she felt about her safety, she said, "I'll be fine."

"It's natural for you to feel scared, you know." He reached out and laid a hand on her shoulder.

"Are you ever scared?" she asked, trying to ignore the heat of his touch through her shirt.

He let out a short laugh. "On this op? Yeah, I'm scared to death."

"That's not encouraging." She let out a short, nerve-filled laugh.

Craig smiled. "Listen, Mary—Can I call you Mary?"

"Sure, go ahead."

His tongue had been in her mouth and he was tasked with keeping her from getting killed for the near future, so why not?

"Mary. It's going to be all right."

"How can you be sure?" she asked, really wondering if he knew something she didn't or if it was just a line to comfort her.

"You're under the care of one of the most highly trained, specialized groups in the US military. Hell, in the whole world. We're not going to let anything happen to you. SEALs don't accept failure as an option."

SEALs?

So that answered *that* question. Craig did know something about the group protecting her that she hadn't known.

No one had bothered to tell her that's who these guys were, but it would have been nice if they had.

However, knowing the level of security surrounding her made her feel less safe rather than more. If the people who'd sent her here felt this much expertise was required to keep her alive—an elite team of highly trained men who were prepared to die defending her—what did that say about how dangerous this job was?

Should she be more afraid than she already was? Were Amanda and Jenny right? Was her life truly in jeopardy?

"That really doesn't help me feel better." She wasn't joking now.

Craig sighed. "It's okay for you to feel scared. You just have to learn how to deal with it."

Oh, yeah. That was real helpful. She scowled. "How have you dealt with it?"

Besides carrying enough weaponry on his body to annihilate most enemies . . .

His eyes narrowed as his gaze held hers. "I'm not sure. This is a first for me—being scared."

"Why? Have you never been here before?" she asked.

"I've been here. I've been lots of places. I'm scared because of you." His tone, his look, his words made her think they weren't talking about the danger anymore, but something else entirely.

"I don't understand."

"I'm not usually emotionally invested in our assignments. This is the first."

She swallowed hard. "Oh."

"Mary, I will die making sure nothing happens to you. I promise you that. My team and I will take care of your safety. All you have to do is figure out a way to focus and do your job."

She swallowed hard. "I guess I'll figure it out. Or we'll figure it out together."

He dipped his head in agreement. "Together sounds good."

Was it her imagination or was he closer than before? His face nearer to hers. His lips right there, almost within reach. Just out of kissing distance.

Craig drew in a deep breath that expanded the breadth of his already wide chest. He had to be thinking the same thing she was—remembering that single kiss. The one she couldn't seem to forget.

The one—if her pounding heart was any indication—she wanted to repeat.

What he—judging by the tip of his head towards hers—wanted to repeat as well.

"Mary?"

"Yes?" Her eyes began to drift closed in anticipation of his lips on hers.

Could she—a serial monogamist—do this? Be with him and not get attached? Be casual and just enjoy herself like her friends kept telling her to?

Right now, as she wanted to feel her lips against his more than all else—she was willing to try.

"The lieutenant needs us back in the war room for a briefing."

His words were like a bucket of cold water the fire of her desire.

Eyes wide open now she pulled back, out of kissing range.

"Oh. Of course. We can go." She glanced around the room. "I have my jacket on. Do I need anything else? Paper and pen?"

His lips tipped up in a smile. "No, professor. Just bring yourself—in your flak jacket."

Saved from herself by Craig's commanding officer. She had yet to decide if she was grateful for that or not.

CHAPTER THIRTEEN

"Lady professor makes body armor and tactical pants look good. Probably not as good as she looks out of them though." Tompkins elbowed Craig in the ribs as they stood in front of the coffee machine. "Right, Dawson?"

Trying hard to hold on to his patience as well as his temper, Craig said, "I told you. Nothing happened. I walked her to her car. She got in, drove away and I left. The end."

He braced himself for more comments but they didn't come.

Tompkins tipped his head to one side as if evaluating the sincerity of Craig and his words. "You're telling the truth, aren't you? You really didn't go home with her."

Craig threw his hands in the air. "That's what I've been trying to tell you."

"Why the hell didn't you go home with her?"

Tompkins frowned.

"I—" He realized he didn't have an answer. "I don't know."

Yes, it had been an arrangement, a fake hook up to start, but he couldn't deny that kiss had felt very real. Things could have easily ended up differently that night if he'd pursued it a little more. Asked her to coffee. Something. Anything.

But he hadn't. He'd walked away with his tail between his legs like a scared puppy.

Tompkins scowled. "You damn kids nowadays. Don't know how to close the deal."

"I do. I can." Even as he said it, Craig realized he'd backed off once again in Mary's living quarters here on base.

He could have easily kissed her and he didn't. And it wasn't for lack of interest on his part either. Or hers, judging by the fact she'd leaned in rather than away.

Why was he such a damn boy scout when it came to women? What was wrong with him?

Tompkins shook his head. "Well, if you're not going for it with her, I might give it a shot."

"What?" Craig opened his eyes wide. "No."

"Why can't I? If you don't want her . . ." Tompkins asked, amusement coloring his tone.

Craig did want her but he wasn't going to say that. He searched for another reason. "It's against the rules."

"She's a civilian, not military, so that doesn't apply."

He scrambled for another reason. "But still, she's under our care."

"And I intend to take very good care of her. Both in and out of our beds." Tompkins followed his crude statement with a wink and a grin.

Craig felt the frown settle over his eyes. Things had gone from bad to worse.

This was what he got for being honest. He would have been better off leaving things alone. But no, that wouldn't have been fair to Mary.

He couldn't have let them continue to think Mary was into casual hook ups with guys she hardly knew, because she wasn't. He could tell that just from what little he knew about her so far.

She wasn't into casual hook ups.

The vise squeezing his heart loosened as he reviewed that thought and absorbed the truth of it. She wasn't into casual hook ups so it didn't matter what Tompkins said or even what he did—she wouldn't fall for it.

Tompkins could try but all he'd do is make a fool of himself when she turned him down. Craig felt like whooping for joy at the realization.

He also realized that his and Mary's relationship was different. It felt as if they really knew each other in spite of the short time they'd been together.

There was a bond. A friendship. A kinship.

When—if—anything happened it wouldn't be a casual thing between them. It would be built, slowly, upon the strong foundation they'd already begun to forge.

And next time she looked at him with those eyes that invited more—by god he was going to take more. When she raised those tempting lips towards his, he was going to take them.

Another glance at Tompkins proved the man was still watching for his response. Craig had to think that half the things Tompkins did and said were just to stir up trouble and see if he could get a reaction.

Chances were the man hadn't even been serious about making a play for Mary. But Craig couldn't worry about Tompkins now. He had to get back to her.

Being with her was his job, but more, he wanted to.

"I gotta get going." Craig turned toward the coffee machine.

He poured a cup full for Mary and then added the cream and two sugars he'd seen her add when she'd fixed herself a cup. After a quick stir, he snapped on the lid and headed outside and toward her living quarters.

Mary had wanted to unpack her stuff. He trusted her to not leave her quarters without him and he'd figured she didn't need him hovering over her shoulder while she settled in. But she should be done by now.

He covered the distance between the chow hall and her trailer quickly enough.

What wasn't so quick was Mary's response to his knock. She didn't respond to his first light tap.

Worried, he pounded louder. Probably a bit harder than was necessary as he second-guessed his own actions. He should have stayed with her. He shouldn't have left her alone.

Hell, he should probably demand command find them adjoining quarters. His being next door, even sharing a wall, wasn't close enough. They needed someplace that anyone wanting to get to her would have to get past him first. That way Craig could better protect her day and night.

He was ready to kick down the door when he heard the lock slide. She looked exhausted as she pulled open the door.

Finally able to breathe again, he pushed past her into the room and closed and locked the door behind him. "Are you okay? You didn't answer right away."

"I was napping."

He could tell the time difference was taking its toll on her. She looked disoriented and adorably sleepy. "I'm sorry I woke you. But you really shouldn't go to bed."

Sleepily, she rubbed her face with one hand. "Why not? I—we—don't have to be at the Institute until tomorrow."

He liked the sound of that *we* but that was not the issue here. "But if you go to sleep now, you'll be up and wide awake in the middle of the night. Then you'll be exhausted by lunch. Trust me on this. I have lots of experience with jetlag. It sucks but the best way to get over the time change is to power through."

A deep frown creased her forehead. She obviously did not like his suggestion. He didn't care. He was so relieved she was all right he could handle her displeasure.

Maybe the coffee would help. He held the offering out. "I brought you coffee."

She pulled her mouth to one side, contemplating caffeine versus sleep he supposed. Finally she took the cup. "Thank you."

He glanced around her room. "So, you settling in all right?"

"Considering I'm in Iraq living inside what amounts to a shipping container on the front line of the war against ISIS? Yeah, sure. I'm settled in great." She cocked up one brow.

His lips twitched. She was waking up if she had it in her to give him that kind of attitude. "The front line is well over an hour's drive from here and it's shifting, moving farther from us. And you'll get used to living in a can. You should be grateful for it, actually. Otherwise you'd be sleeping in a tent like the others are while we're here."

"I won't get used to this coffee." She wrinkled her nose at her first taste and then put the cup down on the desk.

He laughed. "Well, yeah. Probably not—" The siren blaring throughout camp cut him off.

Training and instinct kicked in.

While the others would be running wherever they were needed, taking their posts to protect the camp from whatever had triggered the alarm, Craig's assignment was singular and clear.

Mary Elizabeth.

His sole goal was to protect her and right now, without more information, without knowing what exactly the threat was, the smartest course of action was to shelter in place.

He knocked her to the lower bunk, covering her with his body. It wasn't the ideal location as far as safety went, but it was low and protected from above by the upper bunk's mattress.

"What's happening?" she asked as he felt her shaking beneath him.

"I don't know yet. It could be nothing." Though they usually didn't blow the siren for nothing. He kept that to himself.

"What do we do?" she asked.

"For now we hold tight."

Craig realized he was doing exactly that—holding her tight. His arms remained wrapped firmly around her.

He'd be far more effective if his hands were free to reach for his weapon should a threat come through that door.

In spite of knowing that, he couldn't bring himself to let her go. Not while she was so scared she was shaking.

It probably wasn't more than a couple of minutes that he held her like that in silence before the all-clear signal sounded.

"What's that?" Her continued panic was evident in her voice.

"It's a good thing. The threat's passed." Craig didn't know what that threat had been—he'd find that out later—but whatever it had been had been eliminated.

Mary Elizabeth drew in and blew out a long slow breath. He felt it in the rise and fall of her chest crushed beneath his, reinforcing his awareness of their extreme closeness.

He was still on top of her when there was no further need to be. So why hadn't he moved?

Because he was thinking like a man and not like a combat experienced operator, that's why. He needed to get his head on straight and now.

Bracing his hands on the mattress on either side of her he pushed up and off her . . . but he didn't get too far.

She reached up and with one hand on the back of his neck pulled him back down.

He didn't move in to kiss her, but he didn't move away either. Taken by complete surprise he felt powerless to do anything.

So much for his quick reaction skills and training.

He remained frozen in place above her but he didn't have to move because she did. She leaned up while pulling him down until her lips were against his.

The kiss knocked him out of his stupor. For better or worse, he kissed her back. Deeply and thoroughly.

She sucked in air and pulled him tighter, kissing him with abandon.

Hell, he didn't feel exactly in control himself. Craig angled his head and plunged his tongue into the heat of her mouth.

This was crazy. The situation had gone from deadly serious to sex-starved desperation in seconds but Craig was nothing if not adaptable. He rolled with the changes and kissed her deeper, plunging his tongue against hers.

She broke the kiss and gasped, "Do I have to wear my vest while I kiss you too?"

With his mind reeling from the suddenness of what was happening, it took his spinning brain a beat to realize she was teasing him about the body armor.

"You can take everything off as far as I'm concerned." He'd gladly shield her with his own body while she was naked. In fact, he couldn't wait.

Judging by the flush of her cheeks she hadn't been quite ready for his suggestive comment.

The doubt-filled look in her eyes forced him to tamp down his need for her.

Deep down he'd wanted her since he'd first kissed her in Vegas. They had taken a long, convoluted, round about way to arrive here—in a bed together—but here they were.

But he could see she wasn't ready for that yet. And if the siren hadn't sounded they wouldn't be in bed at all.

Craig drew in a breath and moved off her. "I'm going to find out what that alarm was about. Okay?"

"You're leaving?" Her eyes widened with obvious fear.

"You can come with me if you want, but I'd prefer you stay here. You'll be safer."

"Will you come back?" she asked.

"As fast as I can."

She swallowed hard. "Will you stay in here with me for awhile tonight?"

His heart thundered at the thought of spending the night with her. Of all the things he'd love to do with her. Of all the things he wasn't going to do because the invitation stemmed from fear, not lust.

"If you want me to."

"Yes, please. I'm scared."

Of course, she was. And he was a shithead for not realizing the whole kiss was in response to how shaken she was from the alarm.

What she craved was human contact in the face of fear.

He could give her that.

"You got me for as long as you need me." If that meant he ended up sleeping alone in the top bunk in her can tonight, then so be it. He moved to the door and reached for the knob. "I'll be back."

She nodded and forced a small smile. "Don't take too long. Okay?"

He smiled back, knowing he'd do anything for this woman. "You'll hardly miss me."

CHAPTER FOURTEEN

Craig had snuck out of Mary's trailer before dawn the next morning hoping to avoid being seen.

Even so, he had his cover story rehearsed just in case. He'd say that she was frightened on her first night on base and was afraid to be alone after the alarm so she'd asked him to stay.

The worst part was his *story* was all true. She'd asked him to stay and she had been scared. But it would be just his luck to catch hell for being with her without the benefit of actually having been with her. She'd been exhausted, from travel, jetlag and fear combined. She'd fallen asleep leaning against him in her bottom bunk.

He'd gotten to hold her all night long as she'd slept. It wasn't as fun as what he'd hoped to be doing in that bed but still, he'd loved every minute of it. And then there had been that one kiss. The memories of that had him smiling as he grabbed fresh clothes, and through an early shower, and on the path from the shower trailer back toward their quarters.

The sun was just starting to rise, lighting the sky enough he could see Brody heading his way. Craig tipped his head toward his teammate. "Hey."

"Hey. Grant needs us all on the tarmac now. We got called in."

"What do you mean?" He was scheduled to drive Mary to the Institute.

They were already on an op. An important one as far as Craig was concerned and now, according to Brody, they were getting yanked out?

"There's been a hijacking. A passenger jet. Hundred and thirty on board."

Craig's eyes widened. "And we're being called in for it?"

"Looks like we're the closest unit."

"Shit. I have to tell Mary today is off." She'd just have to start work tomorrow or in a couple of days after he got back.

Brody shook his head. "No, she's still going."

"What? With who?"

"They're sending some of the Army guys with her."

"Army guys weren't included in the planning of this." Craig frowned as that information didn't sit well with him.

"What's up with you?" Brody asked, eyes narrowed as he looked at Craig.

"I don't like the change."

Brody lifted a brow. "Why not?"

"Because we're supposed to be protecting her."

"You've got a thing for the professor." Brody's words came out sounding more like a statement than a question.

"No—" Craig sighed and aborted the denial. It didn't matter. "She agreed to come here based on the fact we'd be here to protect her."

"And she will be protected. Just not by us, Romeo. The Delta guys can handle it. No problem. Unless you're worried she'll fall for one of them while we're gone." Brody grinned, teasing him.

"What? No." Craig frowned.

"Don't worry, kid. We shouldn't be gone long enough for that. You know these hostage standoffs never last too long. Couple of days and we'll be back on base and then you can resume business as usual with the sexy teacher."

Craig let out a breath. "Fine, just let me tell her before we go."

"Dawson, there's no time to say goodbye to your girl. We're wheels up in like five minutes. The transport's waiting. We have just enough time to grab our kits and we're gone."

After one more glance toward the trailer in the distance where Mary was likely sleeping peacefully, Craig blew out a breath. "Okay."

The best he could do was help take down the bad guys on that jet and free those hostages as quickly as they could so he could get back to her. Though after the night they'd had together, the dead last thing he wanted to do was leave her—and without even saying goodbye. But he had no choice.

She'd understand. She had to.

CHAPTER FIFTEEN

The knock on the door of Mary's trailer had her heart speeding. She ran to open it expecting to find Craig. Instead, she found two burly, heavily bearded men with even heavier hardware strapped to their vests.

Definitely not Craig.

She didn't recognize these guys as any of the men she'd met in Nevada who had traveled here with her either.

"Um, hi. Can I help you?" she asked, a bit nervous.

"We're here to escort you, ma'am."

"But Craig, um Dawson, was supposed to escort me. And actually be with me all day at the Institute. As my intern."

One lifted his dark brows. "They didn't say anything about that."

The other nodded. "Right. We have orders to

escort you to the chow hall and then transport you to the Institute, make sure you get safely inside, and then return immediately to base."

In a tag team assault, the other jumped back in and said, "We'll meet you there at seventeen hundred to transport you back here again but that's it. Nobody said anything about staying all day."

"Or about us being an *intern*." One shook his head, looking amused at the idea.

"Oh. Okay." She drew in a breath as concerns flew through her brain. One in particular. Where the hell was Craig?

Flustered, she spun back to glance in her trailer, her mind a blank for a second as her eyes hit on the mattress where she'd spent the night with Craig. Just sleeping, but still, when he'd left her he'd promised to come back.

What the hell was going on that he wasn't here as planned? They were supposed to have breakfast then drive together to the institute with his team following them.

Surely he wasn't avoiding her because of last night. Was he?

They had kissed. Actually, she'd kissed him first, though he'd reciprocated quickly enough. Then he'd spent the whole night with her, holding her.

Was he worried she was getting too close too fast? Was he easing away trying to let her down easy so she didn't get too attached?

She was just insecure enough to wonder.

But he'd left after kissing her goodbye and whispering he'd be back to get her for breakfast at seven.

What could have changed in a few short hours?

Another horrible thought hit her. What if someone had seen him coming out of here after spending the night and he was in trouble? She didn't know much about the military or the rules but what if they'd thrown him in the brig or something?

She needed to find out more.

"Did Craig ask you to take me instead of him?"

One shook his head beneath the helmet. "I don't know any Craig. Our team leader told us to come get you. That's all I know."

"When?" she asked.

"He said to get you here at zero-seven hundred."

Boy, these guys were literal. She reformed her question. "Not when were you supposed to get me. When did your team leader tell you this?"

"About an hour ago." He finally answered the correct question but she didn't like what he said.

It was not too much more than an hour ago that Craig had left her. Something had definitely happened. *Shit.*

Forcing herself to focus, she reached to grab her bag with her notebook inside from where it hung from the top bunk.

She slung it over one shoulder and turned toward the door and the two men standing inside. "All right. I'm ready."

"Flak jacket," one said, tipping his chin toward the vest she'd left hanging on the back of her chair.

The vest's mere presence reinforced in Mary Elizabeth's mind once again she wasn't in Nevada anymore. And now she wasn't even with the one man she knew well enough that she trusted him to protect her.

With a sigh she let her bag slip to the ground.

Her protection for the day wasn't Craig, but apparently they shared his obsession with her wearing her vest.

Scowling, she stalked toward the damn thing.

In spite of keeping her eyes peeled, she didn't see any of Craig's team during breakfast. Nor as they drove in the SUV across base and ultimately through the gate and out into the city of Erbil.

Her first day at the Institute, but she was far less excited about this day than she had been.

CHAPTER SIXTEEN

"Target in sight."

"Hold."

Breathing steadily, slow and shallow, Craig held his position as ordered by his commanding officer.

The sniper rifle might as well be an extension of his body at this point. He'd spent so many hours behind it. Holding it. Cradling it. Like a lover.

While on ops he spent more time with his weapon than anything or anyone else.

He'd use whatever he could find to create a solid perch for himself and the rifle in his chosen sniper hide. He'd end up stretched out on his stomach on rooftops, on the ground, on tables, desks, or doors he'd had to take off the hinges.

The effort was more so he'd be at peak performance, and less to be comfortable. Even so, it didn't hurt when he was set up properly. Then he could concentrate completely on the job without anything tugging at his subconscious.

Though something was niggling at his mind now and it had nothing to do with his position as he kept the hijacker in his crosshairs.

It was Mary Elizabeth as he wondered what she was thinking. He'd spent the whole night with her, holding her. He'd kissed her and promised to pick her up for breakfast and the trip to the Institute and then he hadn't shown.

He didn't know who the hell had filled in for him and the team and he didn't like that. Delta Force or not, this was his assignment and not being able to fulfill it bothered him.

The target moved, putting him behind the fuselage of the jet and out of Craig's sights.

"Target lost." He spoke, knowing his words would filter from his communicator and into the ear of Grant Milton who would relay them to the FBI hostage negotiator.

"Roger that," Grant replied, his voice coming through Craig's earpiece.

After three hours of watching the hijacker move in and out of his scope Craig was ready for this negotiation to go one way or another.

The hijacker could give up, release the hostages and come out with his hands up under his own steam. Or the negotiator could decide the hostages were in imminent danger and order the shot, in which case one dead hijacker would have to be carried out.

Craig didn't care which way it went as long as it was over soon. The motivation to get back to the base in Erbil far outweighed the fact his legs had long ago gone numb from not moving.

"Dawson, you need a break?" Grant asked through the communicator.

"No, sir."

"Take one anyway," the order came back. "Cassidy. Relieve Dawson."

"You got it." Brody's southern drawl filtered through the communicator but the conversation happening in Craig's ear seemed distant.

It took a backseat to what was happening in front of his scope as the hijacker moved again, hovering just inside the doorway and moving in and out of the range of a clear shot.

He finally came into clear view and Craig saw something that had his stomach bottoming out. "Target has hands on a female hostage."

"Can you see a weapon?" Grant asked.

"Knife to her throat."

"Gun? Detonator?"

"No."

"Hold." Grant was no doubt waiting for the negotiator to approve the shot.

Craig tried to remember to breathe as he waited. Muscle memory took over when he actually fired, but those moments leading up to the shot, that was when his brain tried to take over, which wasn't always a good thing.

"You have a clear shot, Dawson?" Grant asked.

"Affirmative." Craig drew in a measured breath and steadied the crosshairs over the man's forehead in his scope.

Shooters were trained to aim for center mass when possible, but that wasn't happening today.

Not with the target holding the hostage against him and the fact they didn't know if he was wearing a suicide vest. It would have to be a head shot.

Not a problem.

He was closer to the target than he usually was. The female the hijacker held was shorter than the man holding her. And to the best of their knowledge this was a lone hijacker so there was no need to take out multiple targets simultaneously.

That would all work in Craig's favor.

Now all he needed was the order . . .

"Dawson, fire at will."

Craig drew in a breath and, smooth and slow, squeezed the trigger. He felt the recoil, absorbing it, before clearing the shell casing and chambering another round. Not that he was anticipating needing it. One was all he needed.

The man fell as the frightened hostage ran from the plane.

Craig blew out the breath. "Target down."

"Target down. Alpha team, move in," Grant ordered.

Operatives located closer ran for the jet to clear the remaining hostages.

Craig held, remaining at the ready. The danger wasn't completely eliminated. There were too many unknowns. Were there explosives on the jet rigged to go off? Was there really only one hijacker or were more hidden among the passengers?

Watching from his perch through the scope as his team did their job he waited for the answers and the all clear.

Behind him, he heard Brody approaching.

"Hey, I'm here. Take a break." Brody planted his rifle and dropped down next to him, sighting his scope on the jet and the action happening in the distance.

Craig disengaged his finger from the trigger and let himself take a deep breath. "Little late, dude. I did all the work for you."

"Bite me," Brody said from behind his scope.

Craig laughed and stretched, his back muscles protesting from going so long without moving.

Now that his concentration was freed up, his body seemed to wake. His stomach let out a loud grumble.

"Hungry?" Brody asked.

"Yeah. Glad this thing is wrapping up." That was for more reasons than food. "Think we'll head right back to base?"

"Don't see why not. No reason for us to hang around here."

"Good." Even so, they were a distance from Erbil, even by air. They wouldn't be back until late.

Brody took his eyes off the scope just long enough to shoot Craig a sideways glance. "Why? Got a hot date or something back on the base?"

He was going to deny it, but thoughts of Mary Elizabeth caused an irrepressible smile he couldn't control. He had to actually wipe the smile from his face with one hand.

Brody's said, "Holy shit, you do."

Craig couldn't let an accusation like that be possibly overheard by his commander through the comm unit.

He frowned at Brody. "Hey, if you're not going

to keep your eye on that jet, I'm going to have to take over."

"I'm watching. They're bringing the hostages out and patting them down. And don't you go changing the subject."

"There's nothing to talk about. I just like the food in the chow hall better than the bag of nasties they're going to feed us in transit, is all."

"Yeah, a'ight. I believe that. Just like I believe Thom is online in the middle of the night *checking his email*, not having video sex with his girl back home. Sure."

Cracking open a bottle of water from his kit, Craig laughed. "Sounds to me like you're jealous."

Brody snorted. "Then you better check your hearing."

"Whatever." Craig enjoyed his rare victory over Brody.

Minutes passed but sooner than Craig could have hoped he heard Grant say, "Wrap it up, boys. We're done here."

At the welcome order, Brody rolled over. "That's it then. You get your wish, Dawson. We're heading back."

Craig tried not to smile but he certainly had gotten his wish. Less than twenty-four hours after they'd left, they'd be back.

Now, if only Mary Elizabeth was there waiting for him—and more importantly not pissed off.

CHAPTER SEVENTEEN

The library at the Iraqi Institute wasn't the biggest or most extensive Mary Elizabeth had ever seen, but considering the fact they were in a war torn country it was impressive and—she was told—growing as donations of texts contributed from other countries trickled in.

But it was the collection of artifacts she'd be studying, kept behind lock and key, that took her breath away. It was more than impressive. It was a dream come true.

She glanced down at the object in her gloved hands now and felt overwhelmed with amazement. It was a near three-thousand-year-old head from a stone sculpture she'd tentatively identified through her research today as being from the palace of Sargon II.

It was thrilling. Invigorating. Humbling. Even working alone in a facility staffed by strangers hadn't deflated the excitement.

More importantly, being engrossed in the work had helped take her mind off the worry and doubt regarding Craig's disappearance.

A knock on the door of the windowless room she was working in brought her head up. "Come in."

The younger man who'd shown her to her workspace what must be hours ago now popped his head in. Sven was a student at the Institute, there from Sweden to study but he'd somehow gotten assigned the duty of playing guide for her today.

"Hi." She smiled at him. "Do you need something from me?"

"No, but there are two men here who said to tell you it's time to go. They're carrying guns. Very large ones."

Mary Elizabeth cringed at the look of concern on Sven's face. She scrambled to explain. "Oh. Sorry about that. The university has me staying on the military base because they were, uh, concerned for my safety. I should have met them upstairs but I didn't realize what time it was."

Apparently the work had also made her lose track of time. That was not entirely her fault. Not only was the work fascinating, but she was used to having her cell phone with her to use as a clock. However, she didn't carry it here since it didn't work in Iraq.

Now she realized how lost she felt without it. The windowless room didn't help.

"Where did the day go?" she asked, forcing a

laugh to lighten the mood.

"That happens here." He nodded. "But it's already getting dark."

Shit. They'd told her they'd wanted to be back on base before dark. Her two escorts were scary enough when they weren't annoyed with her. She could only imagine how displeased they'd be now.

She laid the artifact gently back in its cushioned box. Carefully, she lifted the box with both hands and moved slowly to the wall. She slid it into the cubicle and breathed a sigh of relief once it was back in its place.

One couldn't rush when handling things older than the dawn of Christianity. Her new bodyguards would just have to understand that.

Pulling off the thin cotton gloves, she turned back to Sven. "Okay. Ready."

She grabbed her bag off the top of the file cabinet and moved toward the door.

"Don't forget that." He glanced at the hook on the wall.

She'd forgotten that damn vest again. Good thing her young friend had remembered.

She smothered a curse. "Thanks."

Showing up in the lobby sans flak jacket would have been another black mark against her with the already annoyed guards. She probably shouldn't have taken it off in the first place but she couldn't stand to work in it.

Once she was suitably attired, Sven led her out the door and into the hall.

It was a sizeable facility, so Mary Elizabeth had a few moments to talk to her escort before they reached the lobby. Since she'd worked alone all day, she had a lot of questions.

"Do you know if other researchers will be here? I was under the impression I'd be working with a team. I was especially looking forward to meeting the group from the Hermitage."

"Ah, yes. We were told the Russians were to be here last month, but they haven't arrived yet."

"Really? That's odd. Do you know what happened?" she asked.

He lifted one shoulder. "They don't tell students very much. Which is why we keep our ears open." The attractive young man smiled with mischief in his eyes.

Liking him more and more, she laughed. "Good idea. I'll do the same and let you know if I hear anything."

"It's a deal." He grinned and reached for the heavy door that opened on to the lobby. "Here are your friends."

Friends was a bit of an overstatement but she didn't comment. "Thank you. I'll see you tomorrow?"

"Most likely, yes. I live here in the dormitory so . . ." He shrugged good-naturedly.

"Good. I'll see you tomorrow then. Good night, Sven."

"Good night, Professor Smith."

By the time she turned, she could see her escort was running short on patience but not on weapons or bullets, judging by their guns and the bulging pockets in their jacket and pants.

"We should have left an hour ago." One

scowled.

"Then you should have sent someone to get me an hour ago. I came as soon as I was ordered to." She specifically chose that word—ordered—to reinforce how she felt about being treated like she was their subordinate in the military, even though she was not.

With one man on each side of her, they each took her arm and half led, half propelled her as they strode fast toward the front doors. One broke off and peered outside before signaling the other to bring her forward.

From what she'd seen of the city on the drive there this morning, it had looked safe enough. Nothing eventful had happened. She hadn't seen anyone who even looked like a threat in the streets. At least no one who looked as scary as her current escorts did.

But apparently, they weren't taking any chances.

They hustled her to the vehicle not showing much concern for if they walked too fast for her or pushed her a bit too roughly to get her through the rear passenger door. Luckily she was wearing practical footwear with her newly purchased tactical pants and her borrowed flak jacket.

They were obviously effective in their roles as her bodyguards, but certainly not chatty.

All she wanted to do was talk about the amazing items she had seen today and the work she'd done. The incredible antiquities she'd touched and identified, insuring they'd eventually make it back home to where they belonged once it was safe for them to do so.

With these guys as her only companions, it was obvious she wasn't going to get to share her amazing day any time soon. Sven would have been interested but there hadn't been time to tell him.

Having to keep her excitement bottled up was torture. She was itching to talk. To share with someone. Anyone. But the men assigned to her didn't even glance into the backseat where she sat.

Her one thought as they jerked through the darkening streets of Erbil—the driver alternatingly slamming on the gas and the brake in between blasting the horn—was that Craig would have been interested in what she'd done today.

At least she thought he would have cared—but the question remained why wasn't he here?

The doubt followed her through the journey back to base and through a silent lone meal in the dining hall where the two guys had dumped her.

Once again she wished she could stay at the Institute. Then she'd not only have like-minded people to talk to, she could work late every night.

Hell, since insomnia had been her new normal over the past year, if she was staying at the Institute she could work all night long if she wanted to.

She made a decision right there at the long table in the loud dining hall over her tray of mashed potatoes and meatloaf. If the military didn't have to stick to the original plan, neither did she.

If they could yank away Craig and his team and stick her with two somber faced strangers, then she should be able to choose her own accommodations and move to the Institute.

She pushed down the sick feeling in her stomach

caused by Craig's absence and made a vow to herself to talk to the commander about it tomorrow. If she could find him, that was.

The base was big and confusing. She knew the way to her trailer but that was about it. She certainly couldn't go wandering around asking to see Grant Milton. She supposed she could ask her guards, but they'd said they didn't know Craig so they might not know his commander either.

Angry now at being abandoned—by both Craig and her bearded burly escorts—she vowed that tomorrow she was going to demand she be taken to someone in charge. And if no one would take her then she'd go around the military and speak with someone at the Iraqi Institute.

Where were her guards anyway?

She realized she hadn't seen them since they'd arrived. She glanced around the hall one more time but didn't spot them. She was finished eating and ready to leave, but Craig had said not to walk around alone.

Too bad. Craig wasn't here so she didn't have to listen to him. She didn't need a man—not in her life and not to escort her back to her trailer.

Fueled by determination, Mary Elizabeth stood. She dumped her trash in the can and stowed her tray on the pile.

Striding fast toward the exit, she was nearly there when she heard the shout. Seconds later one of the men assigned to her trotted up.

"Where are you going?" he asked.

"Back to my trailer."

"You're supposed to wait for us."

She lifted one shoulder. "I didn't see you."

The deep frown told her he didn't like that answer. "I was eating."

"Oh. I'm sorry. I'm finished and ready to go. Do you need more time?" she asked, remembering how they hadn't done her the courtesy of asking her the same when they practically dragged her away from the Institute.

Scowling, he shook his head. "Come on. Let's go."

"Okay." Her lips twitched with a smile at the small victory.

CHAPTER EIGHTEEN

It was long past full dark and late by the time the team got back to base. Long after anyone should knock on someone else's door.

All that ran through Craig's mind as he stood outside the trailer staring at it and debating what to do.

Alternatives ran through his spinning brain. He could wait until the morning. Or he could go into his own half of the trailer and make so much noise Mary Elizabeth woke up before he knocked on her door.

To hell with it.

She needed to know sooner rather than later why he'd disappeared an hour after they'd spent an incredible night together.

Or at least she should know as much as he was

allowed to tell.

For the first time, Craig truly appreciated what the guys with girlfriends went through. Getting yanked away with little to no notice. Not being able to say much about their classified missions. Being unable to tell them anything specific regarding travel because it could endanger operational security.

Not that he and she were dating. Nowhere close, but damn he felt as if they were headed that way and fast.

Mary Elizabeth was worth the effort on his part to make this work. The only question was, did she feel the same?

He'd soon find out.

Craig knocked softly on the trailer door at first, and then a little louder.

It took a bit of time but finally he heard movement on the other side of the door. "Mary, it's Craig."

The lock and doorknob jiggled and then she yanked the door open.

"Hey," he said.

"Hey." The mixed emotions showing in the expression on her face told him what her single word hadn't. She looked part relieved, part guarded.

He glanced behind him. No one was around so he said, "Can I come in?"

She nodded and took a step back so he could walk inside and close the door behind him.

"Sorry about today."

"Where were you?" she asked.

Craig took a step forward. In her comfortable

clothes—sweatpants and a T-shirt—she looked soft and vulnerable and he itched to pull her into his arms.

He hated the atmosphere between them as they stood there, her looking guarded, him hesitant. He wanted to touch her. Hold her. Explain everything and then apologize and make love to her.

Yeah, right. In his dreams . . .

Instead he said, "The whole team got pulled away for something. I literally had no time to tell you or I would have. I swear. I'm sorry."

She pressed her lips together in an unhappy line. "Does that happen often?"

"Honestly, it depends." He didn't know how else to answer her. He braced himself for more questions that he probably couldn't answer.

The questions didn't come. In fact she didn't say anything. She only nodded once and, her gaze on him, waited.

"I really am sorry."

"I know." She forced a small smile that didn't reach her eyes.

He would have preferred she throw herself into his arms and kiss him, but for now that smile would have to be enough.

Besides, it felt like he had a dozen questions he wanted answers to. "So, how was today? How was the Institute? What did you do? Did the guys who brought you over stay with you?"

Now she smiled for real. "That's a lot of questions."

"I know. I'm sorry." He lifted a shoulder. "I'm just nosy, I guess. You can tell me to shut up."

"No. Come and sit down and I'll tell you all about it." She moved to one of the few places to sit in the room—the bottom bunk.

Happy with the move, Craig followed and sat next to her.

Beaming, she continued, "It was so amazing. I've been dying to talk to somebody and the two scary guys who brought me home didn't seem the chatty type."

He smiled. *Scary* sounded good to him. The scarier the better to keep her safe. He felt immensely better knowing command had made good on providing proper protection for her in his absence in the form of the guys from Delta.

"Two guys rode in the car with you, but there were more in a second vehicle, right?"

She shook her head. "No. Just them. One car. And they didn't stay. They walked me in and picked me up later."

He kept his opinion on what he felt was lax security to himself rather than scare her.

Meanwhile, she kept talking, animatedly telling him about her introduction to the Institute. ". . . but the most amazing part is in the storage room. It's huge and it's filled with artifacts. When Sven brought me downstairs it was like I was in heaven."

His mind picked up on the many parts of that sentence as he zeroed in on one. "Who's Sven?"

Okay, maybe his priorities were messed up that he was more concerned about this Sven guy and less about the specifics of the room in which she'd spent the day working.

"He's a student at the Institute and I might just

have to make him my intern if you keep disappearing on me. Why? You jealous?" she asked.

He pulled his mouth to one side. "Maybe."

"Good." She smiled as she leaned in and pressed her lips to his.

His body told him to keep quiet, kiss her back and then get them both naked. His mind wasn't as easily swayed. He let himself enjoy a moment of tasting her mouth before he pulled back enough to ask, "This storage room have windows?"

"No."

"Good." That eliminated the risk of bullets. He pressed his lips to hers briefly until another concern had him pulling back again. "Is the level the storage room is on underground?"

"Yes."

He nodded. That alleviated the risk of car bombs crashing in on her. He moved on. "How many doors in the room?"

"You'd really rather discuss the architecture of the Institute instead of kissing me?" She smirked.

"No." He cupped her face in his palms and leaned in but before he closed the final distance he repeated, "How many doors?"

"One. Happy?" she asked.

He'd prefer two exits but he could worry more about that later. For now he was content enough with her answers to get to what he really wanted to do.

"I'll be much happier soon." He smiled and ran his hands down her body.

"I don't know about that." She screwed up her

mouth. "I'm not sure I've forgiven you quite yet for disappearing."

"You could let me make it up to you." He brushed his lips across her throat. "I can be very good at making amends."

Mary Elizabeth cocked up one shapely brow. "Had much practice pissing people off and making up for it, have you?"

He barked out a laugh as the images of what he had in mind conflicted with his childhood memories. "With my parents when I was younger, yes, but that wasn't even close to the way I was planning on making things up to you. If you let me, that is."

While lightly nipping at her neck with his teeth, he moved his hands down to her waist and squeezed.

She paused, as if considering his offer. "I guess I could give you a chance to try, and then decide if I forgive you later."

"Good enough. I'll take it."

As he leaned in, she moved back. "You know, it wasn't just that I was annoyed at you for disappearing without a word. I was really afraid you'd been shipped off or locked up in the brig or something because of me. Because you stayed here last night."

Her concern touched him, even as her use of the term *brig* had his lips twitching with a smile. "For you, I'm willing to risk it."

Her eyes widened. "What do you mean, risk it? I was hoping you'd tell me I was worrying for nothing. Could you be shipped off or locked up for real?"

He wobbled his head. "Eh. Doubtful."

She widened her eyes. "Craig!"

This situation was a gray area as far as he was concerned. Them being together personally, physically, was against his commander's wishes. Craig knew that much from Grant's comment that day at NAS Fallon.

At the moment Craig didn't care too much about Grant or his wishes. And he definitely had no intentions of telling command anything, no matter what happened between them.

He brushed a hand over her cheek. "We're good. I promise. Don't worry, okay?"

She eyed him for a bit and finally nodded. "Okay."

"Good." He had better use for their time together than worrying.

Craig moved closer, more than grateful he had the rest of the night to make good on his promise to make his absence up to her.

He figured he'd better do a good job at it too, just in case they got sent out again, which was always a possibility.

"Can you stay all night again?" she asked.

"Yeah. Sure." Even if it was just to talk and kiss and have her fall to sleep on his arm until it tingled from lack of blood flow, he'd be a very happy man.

CHAPTER NINETEEN

"What do you mean the team isn't there?" Craig paused with his toast half way to his mouth.

Across the table, Mary Elizabeth shrugged. "It's not a big deal. I mean I don't need them to do my research, but it's disappointing. I was looking forward to the camaraderie. And call me vain, but I wanted to be able to say I'd worked on the team with the experts from the Hermitage. But the Russians never showed up."

He'd comfort her over her disappointment later, but right now he needed clarification. "When was the Russian team supposed to arrive?"

"I'm not sure of the exact date. Sven had said sometime last month."

There she was, talking about this Sven guy again. Craig hid his scowl. Even though he had spent last night making out with her until they both fell asleep, he was definitely going to make sure to check this guy out. That would have to be in addition to finding out more about the Russian team who'd never shown up.

"Did anyone say where they went instead of the Institute?" he asked.

"No. Why? Is it an issue?" She frowned before her eyes grew wide. "Oh my God. Do you think something bad happened to them? Like maybe they were kidnapped on their way there?"

He bobbed his head to the side. "That's always a possibility."

In this region anything could happen. But there were plenty of other scenarios too. Like maybe the group of Russians hadn't arrived at the Institute because they were elsewhere, doing other things.

Maybe instead of researching artifacts they were studying coalition troop movements. Secretly gathering Intel.

In times of conflict, there were plenty of groups looking to take advantage of the turmoil to take control. Power. Land. Oil. They were all powerful motivators.

Abandoning her bowl of oatmeal, Mary laid her spoon down. "We need to tell someone. Do something."

"We will." Craig had every intention of doing exactly that but without involving Mary Elizabeth.

"And we need to find out more. I'll ask the people at the Institute to give the commanders here everything they have on the missing team," she continued.

That they couldn't do. At least not outright.

Craig shook his head. "No. I'm supposed to be your intern. And you're supposed to be here by arrangement of your university not on behalf of the US. Remember?"

"That brings up a very good question. Why am I here on behalf of the government or the military or whoever?" She pinned him with a stare.

"Because we want to make sure those working on the recovery and restoration of the antiquities are safe." He hated doing it with every fiber of his being, but he had no choice, so he lied.

Or at least stretched the truth since it wasn't completely a lie. He was there to keep Mary Elizabeth safe, but she was there not just to research artifacts.

She was really there as the team's cover. Their excuse for being in the country and keeping an eye on what was happening in the region.

Between Russian, Turkish, Syrian, Kurdish, Iraqi and Coalition troops, there were too many players on the field currently to not have operatives in place—just in case.

"So we can't help the missing Russians because you're supposed to be a grad school intern and not a sailor or a SEAL or whatever the hell you are— which you never outright told me, by the way." She finally drew in a breath at the end of the long rant and Craig realized he really had kept her in the dark about a lot of things.

Obviously she wasn't handling that fact very well. Admittedly, their nightly sleepovers and make out sessions weren't helping the situation.

He glanced around the immediate area and then leaned forward.

Keeping his voice low he said, "As soon as you're done eating we'll go to the commander and tell him about the Russian team. You can also make inquiries at the Institute but only as a concerned colleague. And since it's not a secret that you're staying here on base instead of at the Institute, maybe we can offer to inform someone here about the team and provide assistance in a search. We can get it all accomplished. We just have to be careful how we do it. Got it?"

She pressed her lips together. "Yes."

"You don't look happy."

"It's a lot. I teach for a living. This—this hiding things and lying and body armor and armed guards—it's a lot."

"I know it is. But that's why I'm here. To help." He saw his team heading their direction and tipped his head. "And also why they're all here."

Holding his breath, Craig waited for the guys to join them. His team and Tompkins' team would be alternating days, taking turns being in the follow vehicle.

He didn't know which crew made him more nervous. Brody, who insisted on teasing him about Mary Elizabeth. Or Tompkins, Clyde and Fitz, who had been there for that whole screwed up *Dare for a Dime* night in Vegas.

Being around either group of guys was not ideal, but there wasn't a whole lot Craig could do about it. Especially not now as, grinning, Brody pulled out a chair and sat.

"Mornin', professor. You sleep well last night?" Brody cut Craig a sideways glance before focusing back on Mary Elizabeth, whose cheeks flushed at the question.

Craig jumped in to save her. "It's her first experience sleeping in a can so I wouldn't expect her to be used to it quite yet."

Brody nodded solemnly. "Ah. True, true. Hard to get used to those cans. Maybe they should move her to the tent where we're all staying. Though, you're in the can with her, aren't you, Dawson?"

Craig was inspired to kick Brody's cocky ass, or at least give him a nice bruise in the shin with his combat boots. He controlled the impulse and said, "In the one *next* to hers. For safety."

Brody nodded again. "Right. Best to be safe."

Judging by the smirks on the faces of Rocky and Thom, Brody had shared his theory about Craig's feelings for Mary. They remained standing, arms folded as they watched the show before them.

Craig would have to *thank* Brody for sharing later—possibly with a punch in the gut next time they sparred during training.

Mack strode up to the table. "I brought the second vehicle around. It's parked up front. You ready to go, Dawson?"

At least Mack was staying on task. Unlike Brody.

Unfortunately, even with as much as Craig would like to get into that SUV alone with Mary and be away from the rest of these clowns, there was something they needed to do first. "About that. Mary just told me something we need to bring to command's attention."

"What did *Mary* say, Dawson?" Brody asked, looking amused at Craig's use of her first name.

Craig ignored that and said, "That there was supposed to be a team of Russian experts at the Institute but they never showed up when expected."

That tidbit sobered Brody up fast enough. The guys exchanged glances but no comments. They were all too aware there was a civilian in their midst.

"I'm worried they were kidnapped and taken hostage or worse, like those aid workers and reporters I've seen on the news who were killed. *Beheaded*." She whispered the last word.

Obviously concerned, Mary Elizabeth had gone pale as she spoke about the horrors the whole world had seen thanks to the internet and the media.

He itched to comfort her. To reach out and take her hand in his. Tell her he'd kill or die to make sure nothing bad ever happened to her.

Craig couldn't do any of that so he said, "If any of that had happened we'd have heard already. Or seen the video. The bad guys like to broadcast their deeds. They see no benefit in keeping things secret."

Judging by her horrified expression, his words hadn't comforted her as intended.

"We'll swing by the head shed on the way off base and tell command. They'll look into it. A'ight?" Brody focused on Mary.

"Okay. And we can ask for more details at the Institute too. That way we can tell your commander more when we get back tonight. Right?" Mary turned to Craig.

She looked so excited to be helping and involved, Craig couldn't help but smile. "Yes, we can."

Brody's gaze moved between the two of them. "Well, it looks like you and the kid here have a full day ahead of you. I guess we'd better get moving."

"I'm ready." She stood fast and grabbed her bag, flinging it over her shoulder.

"So I see. Let's go." Brody sent him another glance. Craig didn't miss the smirk.

CHAPTER TWENTY

Mary Elizabeth, with Craig flanking her and walking more like a guard than an intern, had barely cleared the front doors when a suited dark-haired man trotted across the lobby.

She recognized him as the director from his photo on the Institute's website.

"Professor Smith." He ran forward and took both of her hands in his. "I'm so sorry I wasn't here to greet you yesterday on your first day with us. I was traveling and it couldn't be helped."

"Please, think nothing of it. Sven was an excellent tour guide. He showed me everything."

"I'm glad. I can't tell you how much we appreciate your taking time away from your classes at the university to be here with us. We're so thrilled you joined us."

"Thank you for having me. It's an experience of a lifetime. I wouldn't have missed it for anything in the world. Your facility is amazing and the collection of antiquities—the storage room alone took my breath away when I first walked in. All the artifacts . . ." She shook her head, unable to come up with the words to describe it.

He laughed. "Ah, a kindred spirit, I see. I felt the same my first day. I still do. Perhaps we should form a support group and meet in the evenings to discuss it."

"Perhaps." She laughed his suggestion off as a joke.

Next to her, Craig let out a soft humph. She ignored him, secretly enjoying he was jealous.

"I'm sorry. I'm being rude. Let me introduce you to my intern . . ." She stumbled over the introduction not knowing if Craig was supposed to have a fake name to go along with his fake internship.

What did she know about all this military intrigue? He should have gone over this with her. She counted on him to lead her in this situation.

Tongue-tied and panicked, she turned to Craig and hoped he saw the question in her expression.

Smiling, cool and calm, he stepped forward, hand extended. "Nice to meet you, sir. Craig Dawson. I'm Professor Smith's intern."

"Very nice to meet you as well. What an opportunity for you to be working not only with the professor, but on such an amazing project."

Craig nodded. "Yes, sir. It certainly is an honor."

"So, I'll let you two get to work. But if there is

anything I can do for you or if you have any questions—"

"Actually . . ." she began.

He raised a brow. "Yes?"

"Sven had mentioned that the Russian team was supposed to be here already. I was just wondering, given the volatile conditions in the region, should we be concerned that something has happened to them?"

"Oh, goodness no. They checked in with me to say they had a change of plans and their arrival would be delayed. They said they'll be touring some of the sites on their way here."

"Oh, really? How wonderful for them to get to go on site. I mean the collection here is amazing and fascinating, but . . ."

"It doesn't match the excitement of walking in the footsteps of those who walked there thousands of years ago? Yes, you're right. But not to worry. We have some significant sites right here in Erbil. We can take—how you say—a field trip. In fact, we're very proud that our Citadel was added to UNESCO's World Heritage List in 2014."

She smiled. "A field trip sounds wonderful. We'd love that. Thank you. Do you know where the Russian group will be visiting? Just so I can be suitably jealous of them until I can tour the sites myself, of course."

He mirrored her smile. "I believe they're using the map of sites in danger that The Antiquities Coalition has compiled. If you haven't visited that organization's website, you really should. It's truly amazing."

She nodded. "I definitely shall. And now I'd better let you go. You have more important things on your schedule, I'm sure."

"None more important than you. But you're anxious to get back to the collection, I'm sure. Perhaps I'll see you in the cafe for lunch later?"

"I hope so." Relieved to know the team was safe, and equally happy that the director hadn't glanced twice at Craig and didn't seem suspicious at all, Mary Elizabeth was happy to get back to work with a clear head.

As the director ascended the staircase from the lobby to the offices above, she turned to Craig. "The stairs to the storage room are this way."

"Is there a computer in there with an internet connection?"

"Yes, of course. That's how I did my research yesterday. There are plenty of documents and texts in the Institute's database but I still needed a few things off the web." She talked as they walked, although he didn't seem to be listening as intently as usual.

They arrived downstairs at the door of the storage room and she keyed in the code she'd been given to release the lock.

"Who else has access to this room?" he asked, all business.

"I don't know."

He nodded and stalked into the room the moment she opened the door and flipped on the lights. He moved directly to the computer.

"I wouldn't assume this is secure so don't do anything on here you wouldn't want anyone else to have. No passwords. No logging into email." He shot her a glance. "Okay?"

"Um, okay." She hadn't even considered that her online usage could be monitored but now that he'd said it, it made a certain paranoia-inspired sense.

They were in a foreign country and rules were different here. The government could monitor anything they pleased, she supposed.

Luckily she'd been too excited yesterday to dive into her research. She hadn't bothered to worry about her probably overflowing email inbox.

He brought up a browser as she stepped to his side. "What are you doing?" she asked.

"Trying to bring up that website he was talking about. The organization with the map. While I'm doing this, you might want to tell me what UNESCO is so I don't have to pretend that I know next time."

"United Nations Educational, Scientific and Cultural Organization. They've compiled a World Heritage List of significant sites."

"Okay. Thanks. I'll look them up later." He typed in a few more things that brought up a search page. He scanned the results. "Got it."

Triumphantly he clicked on a link and theantiquitiescoalition.org home page loaded.

Craig navigated to an interactive map of ancient sites with reported incidents of damage.

He zoomed in on the sites nearby and let out a slow whistle.

She leaned in to take a closer look at all the dots delineating cultural losses and had to agree with Craig's reaction. There were a lot of them. Too many.

He straightened. "All right. I need to go tell the guys about this so they can radio it in to command. You'll be okay here for a bit alone?"

"Yes. You're leaving?"

"I'm not going far. The other vehicle should be parked right outside. I'll let them know and then be right back. Okay?"

"Sure. I can always call for Sven if I get lonely." She couldn't resist the dig.

He cocked up one brow and paused with his hand on the doorknob. "Yeah, don't do that. Okay?"

Her lips twitched with a smile. "Okay. Go tell the guys. I'm sure your command will be relieved to know the Russians are safe and accounted for. I don't want them to worry for nothing."

"Yeah. They'll want to know . . . so they don't worry." He strode forward and pressed a quick hard kiss to her mouth. "You did good up there. You asked the right questions perfectly and got the exact answers we needed."

"Thank you. I'm glad I could help. And I enjoyed my reward." She smiled.

He kissed her again much too briefly. "All right. Enough of that. Gotta go. I'll be right back. Don't leave this room. Okay?"

"Yes, sir." She restrained herself from attempting another salute since she never got her lesson after the first time and watched him leave after another backward glance.

Once he was gone, she moved to the computer and sat in the desk chair. The site was still up in the browser window so she navigated from the map they'd looked at together, to another one. This one of ancient sites overlaid with the areas the terrorists controlled. Places with the potential threat of incurring losses.

There were too many of those too, impressing upon her that in spite of the importance of what she was here to do, there were other factors at play.

Her job of restoring the damage was important, but someone had to stop future damage and destruction from happening in the first place. And that was beyond her power.

With a deep sigh, she stood and moved to the shelves hoping work would raise her spirits, because looking at those maps and sure dampened them.

CHAPTER TWENTY-ONE

On his way out of the building, Craig stopped to talk to the guard in the lobby. It would look less suspicious if he offered an excuse for his quick departure and then imminent return.

As American scholars they were guests at the Institute and of this country. The last thing he wanted to do was jeopardize their cover. He didn't want anyone there to notice him acting oddly or worse, guess he was running information outside to another party, even if that was exactly what he was doing.

"Hey, I gotta run outside to grab something I forgot outta the car. But I'll be right back in. Okay?"

The Iraqi guard barely nodded in response to Craig's lie. He was too busy watching something on his cell phone.

Craig didn't know what the man was so engrossed in. Porn. Funny cat videos. The World Cup.

He honestly didn't care what it was. All the guard's inattention did was make Craig happy he was here to protect Mary Elizabeth since the Institute's hired security was obviously lacking.

Maybe the absence of the security guard's enthusiasm stemmed from boredom because nothing bad had ever happened here.

He couldn't take solace in that theory. Craig would love to but he knew better. He knew from experience that simply because nothing bad had happened in the past didn't mean it wouldn't happen in the future. Especially here.

Outside the building, Craig trotted across the courtyard. He'd feel better once he got this done and got back to Mary Elizabeth.

On the street, he walked to the corner and turned.

There, right where they'd coordinated in advance, he spotted the team's SUV parked. The proximity to the building and the location on the corner offered the team inside the SUV a view of the parking lot entrance and two side streets.

He reached for the back door handle and tugged the door open.

Brody twisted in the driver's seat to be able to see Craig where he stood in the open door. "Hey, it's Casanova. What are you doing out here so soon?"

"Maybe he finally asked out the hot teacher and

she shot him down." Rocky, glancing back from the front passenger seat, grinned

"Yeah, okay. Whatever." Craig lifted a chin toward Thom. "Hey, move over so I can sit. I got something."

Frowning, Thom slid toward the center of the back bench seat, closer to Mack to make room for Craig. Even then, there was barely enough space for him to sit.

Three big guys in the back of a civilian SUV was a tight fit, but that couldn't be helped right now. Craig needed to tell them what he and Mary Elizabeth had learned. The team needed to call it in to command on a secure line.

Craig sure as hell couldn't make the call himself from inside the Institute where any communications could be intercepted and monitored.

"What d'you got?" Mack asked, leaning forward to see past Thom.

"Well, according to the director of the Institute, it seems our missing Russian team of experts are touring the Middle East."

Brody frowned. "Touring where, exactly?"

"That's the part that gets tricky. You got a laptop in here with you?" It was easier for Craig to show them than tell them.

"Yeah." Thom whipped a military grade, satellite enabled, secure laptop out from the seat back pocket.

Once he was connected, Craig typed in the URL and brought up the map from the website. He turned the laptop so the other guys could see the screen

"Apparently, according to the director, the Russian team said they'd had a change of plans. That they'd be visiting some of the locations listed on this website on their way here. At least that's what they told him."

Thom stared at the many dots on the map on screen. "The director couldn't narrow it down a little?"

Craig had already discounted that the director knew any more than he'd passed on. "If they gave him a specific location he didn't share it with us. But my instinct tells me he wasn't lying or holding anything back."

"Hell, it doesn't matter." Brody snorted. "Even if they gave him their damn itinerary, it doesn't mean they're not lying."

"I know, but at least it would have been a place to start. The Russians could be at any one of these sites. Or none of them." Thom shook his head. "Either way, that's a lot of locations for Intelligence to follow up on."

Rocky drew in a breath. "It's really a perfect cover for them. All the hotspots politically also happen to be sites containing antiquities. Pretending to be experts allows them to move freely through the region with a plausible excuse."

Mack laughed. "Yeah, it's a perfect cover, which is why we're using it too."

"Hey, at least we have an actual expert with us. We don't know that they even have that," Rocky pointed out.

Brody lifted one shoulder. "Who knows? They

might. It don't matter a hill of beans anyway. They ain't here and we don't know where they are."

"Command should be able to track them down though. Right?" Craig asked. "I mean a group of Russians moving through Iraq or Syria? They should be on the radar of any eyes and ears we have on the ground."

"We can hope." Brody reached into the console and pulled out a satellite phone. "So, who wants to break the good news to Grant? Any volunteers?"

Craig did not raise his hand, but being the inside man he'd probably have to do it anyway. No one else was going to volunteer because this was definitely not good news.

CHAPTER TWENTY-TWO

The quick knock on the door before it swung open knocked Mary Elizabeth out of her concentration.

She was half expecting to see Craig there. How long had he been gone anyway? Once again, she'd been so engrossed with her work she wasn't sure of the time.

But it wasn't Craig. Instead the director popped his head around the door.

"May I interrupt?" he asked.

"Of course. Come in."

"I have good news, professor."

"Yes?"

"You'll have help shortly. I just received a phone call from the team we discussed this morning. Funny how things go, yes? We speak of them and," he snapped his fingers, "they appear. Like magic."

"It is quite an amazing coincidence. But I'll be happy to have them here. Did they say when they'll arrive?"

"Yes. They are en route. They said most likely they will arrive this afternoon. No later than this evening if they are delayed."

"That's wonderful. I'll look forward to meeting them. And working side by side with them too."

Though she'd have to shelter Craig as much as possible. Experts would be able to see right through his cover and know he was no art history grad student.

Maybe she could give him some busy work that would keep him isolated for a while. Sorting. Cataloging. Something easy that would keep him away from the Russians.

He was not going to like that, she knew.

Too bad. Craig might be able to boss her around on base, even around here when it came to safety and maintaining his cover story, but she was the antiquities expert.

If he wanted to keep up the sham of being her intern—for whatever secretive reason the military was insisting on him appearing to be that rather than a SEAL—he'd have to take direction from her.

She had a feeling she was going to enjoy being in charge.

"I look forward to finally being able to meet them as well," the director said, bringing her mind back to the conversation and away from thoughts of Craig.

"You've never worked with them before?" she asked.

"No. To date we've only spoken briefly on the phone." He wandered closer to gaze upon the piece of sculpture in front of her. "I see you've chosen one of my favorites to work on."

"I swear it was like it called to me from the shelf. The moment I saw it I knew I wouldn't be happy working on anything else before this one." She laughed. "Does that sound strange?"

The older man smiled deeply, wrinkling his eyes further. "Not at all. I feel the same about so many of the items. If only the administration of this wonderful institution took less time and allowed me the leisure to get my hands dirty, so to speak, I'd be a very happy man. But it's what they hired me to do—paperwork—so I do what I must and live vicariously through you."

"I'm happy to share my findings with you."

"And what have you found today? I must admit I've already read over your notes from yesterday in the database."

"That's what they're there for." She moved back to allow him to get closer. "Today has just begun so I'm afraid I don't have a whole lot to tell you—except for this. It appears there's more. Not just the head survived. I think there might be portions of the body that survived as well."

"What makes you think so?"

"I remembered reading about the discovery of a cache of recovered artifacts. I just looked it up on the internet and found photos. The estimated age.

The coloring. The form. It all fits. Look for yourself."

He leaned low and squinted at her screen to look at the portion of stone torso in question. "Amazing. Where is this piece located?"

"It's being held for safekeeping with the collection from the Iraqi Museum. I hesitated to contact them myself, but I thought perhaps you might?"

"Of course. I'd be honored to make the call. I'll try to get in touch with them today and get back to you the moment I do."

"Thank you. Do you think they'll want us to send the head to them?" She felt saddened at the thought of losing her prized piece—her discovery—to another facility.

"I don't know, but let's see if I can get them to ship their piece to us. Shall I?"

She laughed. "That'd be great. Thank you."

"My pleasure. I'll let you get back to your work." As the director pulled the door open, Craig strode down the hall. The director nodded to him on his way out.

Craig closed the door and turned to her. "You didn't say anything about my calling in the possible locations of the missing Russians, did you?"

She frowned. "No." She hadn't even thought about it, not with the exciting news from the director taking all of her attention.

"Good. Don't."

"I really don't understand why—"

"Mary Elizabeth. Please. You have to trust me.

And I have to be able to trust you to not—"

"I know. I know. Jeez, what happened out there?" She didn't understand why he'd left excited and come back cranky.

"Command's not happy with the team touring around. That's all."

"Because it's so dangerous. I understand that. But I found out something while you were gone." Maybe the news would get that accusatory tone out of his voice. "They're on their way here now. The Russians will be here this afternoon."

He widened his eyes. "Today? Seriously? Wow. Okay. I need to—"

"Go and tell the guys. I get it. Go ahead. I'm fine."

"You're more than fine." He smiled and moved closer. Kissing her much too quickly, he pulled back and said, "Sorry I was short with you. It's just so important."

"I know. Go." She smiled.

"I'll be back as soon as I can. Don't go anywhere."

"I know." She was getting pretty tired of the orders.

It just made her look forward to telling Craig what to do once the Russians arrived. Although, once they did, there'd be no more kissing in the storage room.

Hmm. As much as she wanted to work with the team, she was going to miss his quick kisses during her workday. She should be more careful what she wished for.

164

CHAPTER TWENTY-THREE

Craig's eyes had gone blurry long ago. He wasn't sure what he'd done to piss her off but it must have been something, because Mary Elizabeth had given him the worst job on earth to do.

Even the arrival of the three men who comprised the missing Russian team didn't alleviate his boredom. To protect his cover, Mary Elizabeth had introduced him to them and then immediately she'd stuck him in this tiny file room all alone.

He would have rather observed them for a while but she was so afraid his complete lack of historical knowledge would be obvious to them and compromise him, he couldn't argue with her.

The team working in the storage room was being covered without his presence since he'd hidden a small communicator there so the unit in the car outside could record and translate anything the Russians said. So now his task was to sort through every one of the Institute's papers and pull out anything that had to do with this old stone head she was working on.

All the training he'd gone through in the Navy hadn't prepared him for this paperwork bullshit. Now he was sure why he'd tried out for the SEALs—it was to avoid being a desk jockey because he sucked at this shit.

If he ever got assigned desk duty he'd lose his sanity. The past hour was proof of that.

Had it really only been one hour of this torture? He checked his watch again and proved his fears correct. Every hour of paperwork felt like seven.

How much longer until this day ended? Another hour? He wasn't sure he was going to make it.

Sighing, he stretched his back, feeling the stiffness there. Funny how he could lay in a sniper hide for hours before he felt as sore as he did after one hour of shuffling papers.

"Hey." Mary Elizabeth's appearance in the doorway was like a gift from the heavens.

"Hey." He jumped up, happy for the excuse to stop working and even happier to see her, even if she had been the one to assign him this shit job.

"Something's not right." Her somber expression reinforced her words.

"What do you mean?" he asked, concerned.

Shit. What was going on while he was trapped in the file room?

"I showed the Russian team my discovery. I

mean it's exciting. At least to me it was, to be working on a three-thousand-year-old head. But while we were talking about it, one of them made a mistake. The guy who is supposed to be the senior member of the team misquoted the age."

Craig frowned. "Is it possible it was a language thing? Perhaps his English isn't very good."

She wobbled her head. "It's possible if it was just the date and he'd mistranslated it, but he got the location wrong too. The name of the city where this sculpture came from should be the same in Russian as it is in English. He named a completely different one."

"Okay, yeah. That's different." Craig blew out a breath, absorbing this information and trying to reason it out. "Is this Sargon II sculpture you're working on something that's well known in your field or something obscure? Don't be angry when I say this but maybe he just didn't want a woman to know more about something than he does. He could have been spouting facts to try and look like he was more knowledgeable than you, but he got it wrong."

"I wouldn't get angry. I know the glass ceiling is still firmly in place. And I know there are cultural differences as well. But . . . I don't know . . . Since I've been watching more closely there have been a few tiny things that are just off. Most people wouldn't notice. I wouldn't have noticed if I wasn't watching. It's the same reason why I stuck you back here to work today. Away from them so they didn't pick up on the fact that you're not really studying this field. I mean a few mistakes would be expected of an intern but too many and they'd be suspicious."

"And they made too many mistakes." It was clear to Craig that Mary Elizabeth had picked up on something important.

She nodded. "Yes. Exactly. They know some things but they're not the experts they're supposed to be. It's almost like they studied just enough to pass as experts in this specific region, but beneath what they learned there is no foundation. No basic knowledge. And no broad advanced knowledge."

Her discovery put her in a very precarious position, even if she didn't realize that. Craig needed to keep her safe. Warn her without scaring her.

"Did you call them on it? Correct them?" he asked.

"No. I guess I was too shocked at the time. And deep down, I was starting to question my own accuracy. So I went to the computer and double checked. They're definitely wrong. But I didn't tell them that. I didn't think it would make for very good working relations on our first day."

"You did the right thing."

"But what now?" she asked.

"Don't get into specifics with them. Do not question them and definitely do not challenge them."

"Craig, what's going on?"

"We're gonna figure that out. Until then please just pretend it's business as usual and you're happy to be here, working with them. Do not act suspicious."

"Okay."

"And don't be scared."

"I can't help it."

"I know. It's okay. Just try not to show it, all right?"

She blew out a breath. "Easier said than done. Any other instructions?"

"Try not to talk to anyone while I leave to run outside for a second."

"I knew you were going to say that."

"And kiss me quick before I go. Did you know I was going to say that too?" He raised a brow.

"No."

"Good. Don't want to become predictable." He pulled her close and kissed her hard and quick, but even as he tried to lighten the mood, the enormity of her discovery weighed on him.

CHAPTER TWENTY-FOUR

What would be Mary Elizabeth's second day at the Institute working with Craig and the Russians dawned bright and sunny. Unfortunately, her disposition did not match the weather.

Her fear that Craig's lack of knowledge would be discovered by the Russians now took second place to her suspicions about the Russians themselves.

She felt disappointed. Betrayed. More, she was scared. If these three men weren't the experts they claimed to be, who were they?

Was one—or all three of them—really Russian military pretending to be art historians just like how Craig was US military and pretending to be her intern? And if so, why?

The whole mystery had drained her of her

enthusiasm and not just for her work. Last night she'd sent Craig to sleep in his own side of the trailer for the first time since her arrival.

He hadn't commented on the change but she was sure he'd wondered about it.

This morning, they'd eaten their breakfast with not much more than small talk before different men had joined them and followed them to the Institute.

Outside the front door, Craig glanced at her. "You okay?"

"Yeah. Fine."

He considered her for a moment before finally opening the door. They'd barely entered the lobby when the director came down the stairs, but today, he was not smiling.

"Professor." He met her in the middle of the room. "I have sad news."

"What happened?"

"What hasn't happened? Everything has changed since yesterday. Our friends have had to return to Russia. They left late last night. And even more saddening than their loss is the email I received this morning requesting I arrange safe transport of our prized sculpture so the head can be rejoined with the torso."

She didn't know what to comment on first as questions and emotions swirled through her.

The one thought that dominated the rest was that everything was her fault.

She'd brought the possibility of the head and the torso being from the same sculpture to the director's attention. She'd encouraged him to contact the other institution.

Its loss was her fault.

She had been the one to doubt the Russians' expertise. Perhaps they'd sensed her suspicions yesterday.

Now they too were gone.

"I'm so sorry."

"As am I." He tipped his head. "But we go on. You will find a new project to inspire you downstairs."

"Yes. I will. Thank you for telling me. I'll work on choosing the next piece now."

"Good. We will forge ahead. I look forward to seeing what you choose." He nodded his goodbye and turned toward the staircase.

She glanced toward Craig. She could see his brain working, processing the new information just like she was trying to.

"Ready to get started?" she asked him.

"Actually, once I get you settled downstairs I need to run to the car."

"Why?"

He raised a brow but didn't answer her question. Instead, he said, "Let's get downstairs."

The moment the door swung closed behind them she turned to him. "What's going on?"

He pressed his lips together. She knew he didn't trust the computers to be secure here but she was starting to wonder if he feared the room was bugged as well.

Glancing around her, she wondered if there were cameras watching them. Given the value of the items in the room, it was very possible.

She probably should have considered that before, because if so, they'd witnessed her and Craig kissing more than once.

Or maybe this assignment was just starting to make her paranoid.

Either way, she wanted an answer from Craig. Finally, he said, "I just think such a sudden departure is important enough to mention."

She sighed, tired of the intrigue. "You're right. It is. Go."

"You're not okay." His words weren't a question.

"Nope."

"I'm sorry they're taking your head away from you." He pulled her into a one armed hug.

"So am I." She pulled back and gathered her composure. "I'm going to see what else is in here. Maybe I'll find something even better."

"Good. When I get back we'll look together."

"Okay."

When he left her she leaned heavily on the desk. For the first time since walking into this room, she wasn't excited to be there.

Her malaise lasted through the day to the point she finally asked Craig if it was possible that they leave early. With both vehicles and the follow team already there, it wasn't a problem.

They arrived back on base early in the afternoon. Since they hadn't eaten since breakfast he forced her to eat a late lunch. That was fine with her. She figured she could skip dinner and go right to bed.

She liked the plan better and better as Craig walked her from the dining hall to the trailer.

Inside her door he hesitated. "Are you okay?"

"No. I'm sad." She felt like a pouty child but she couldn't help it.

"I know." He pulled her into a hug. While holding her tight he said, "It sucks you lost your favorite project and it sucks the Russians were dickheads."

She laughed. "Yeah."

"I'm sorry you're sad."

"Thank you." His sweetness made her less so. In fact, for the first time since that morning, she felt a bit lighter.

His hugs were magic. So were his kisses. And that could be exactly what she needed.

"Will you stay with me tonight?" she asked.

"Of course."

"Can we maybe not just sleep this time?" She felt him react to that. It was almost like he stopped breathing for a moment before he pulled back and looked into her face.

"Yeah, I think that's a good idea."

She was happy he didn't question her decision or ask why now and why not before, because she didn't have the answer. She was glad he was smart enough to be happy and just go with it.

She waited, her gaze on him.

Finally he leaned in and kissed her, soft at first, but that didn't last long. It soon turned passionate, stealing her breath away and taking her mind off her day while chasing away her sadness.

Craig was a SEAL, fast and expeditious when required. She knew he could be ready for action on a moment's notice. Now he used his skill to undress both himself and her in no time.

Each item he removed from her body ramped up her need for him more. As the pile of clothes on the floor got larger, her desire for him blazed hotter.

When he'd cleared all the obstacles between them and could finally get his hands and his mouth on her, her heart was pounding as hard as if she'd run a marathon. She ran her hands over his warm bare skin.

"We don't have to be anywhere anytime soon, do we? No meeting with your commander? No super secret task that you have to disappear to do?" she asked in a breathy voice.

"Nope. Nothing scheduled until zero-seven-hundred tomorrow."

"Good." She barely got the word out before his mouth covered hers again, taking it with a hard kiss that mirrored all of her own pent up need finally about to be unleashed.

Craig traced his fingers across her skin. His mouth traced the same path, blazing a trail of heat followed by a tingling chill.

She was having trouble focusing on any one thing as her mind skipped around. It roamed from the smoothness of his skin, to the hard bulk of his lean muscles, to the feel of the razor stubble on his face as it scratched against her, to the throbbing caused by his fingers on spots that had gone too long without being touched.

Not being able to think was a good thing. If she couldn't think, she couldn't over-think this either. Couldn't obsess and second-guess and doubt what they were doing.

Maybe her friends were right—she needed this. Needed to touch and be touched by another human. No strings attached.

He was here. She was here. She liked him. He liked her. That was enough.

Hell, he was willing to die to protect her. That's more than any man had offered her in the past, even those who'd proclaimed love and promised her a future.

She tugged her mind off that painful memory with renewed assurance that this with Craig was right.

They didn't have to date. Didn't have to fall in love. No relationship meant no eventual end of that relationship. No conflict or pain. No beginning meant no ending.

This thing between them could be so simple if she just kept it physical with him. Convenient. Temporary.

Could she get her mind to accept that after the heat of the moment had passed? When she was alone in the dark staring at the ceiling and her traitorous brain started to spin with doubts and questions?

She had to. They had to be just a man and a woman enjoying some physical contact together. Nothing more than—

He cut off her thought by slipping his hand

between her thighs and spreading her legs wide.

His eyes dropped to take in her nakedness as his fingers worked her until she trembled. When she was ablaze with sensation, he pulled back his hand.

Moving over her, he positioned himself at her entrance and locked his gaze on hers.

Never taking his focus off her face, he pushed inside.

She was more than ready for this. He slid in easily, sending a wave of relief through her.

He squeezed his eyes shut and hissed in a breath, obviously as overwhelmed with sensation as she was. Her own lids drifted closed as she absorbed every nuance while he loved her.

With every touch, he drove out the darkness that had settled inside her.

The heartbreak, still a shadow hanging over her, seemed to recede just a bit more. She tried desperately not to compare Craig and her ex, but holy hell she couldn't help the comparison.

Whether it was from his age or that he was in top physical condition or just that he was more enthusiastic than Rob ever had been, making love with Craig blew being with Rob right out of the water.

She pushed the fleeting thought aside as she felt her body tighten around his, building toward what she hoped would be her first orgasm in much too long.

When it broke over her, she tried her best to stifle the cries that escaped her. She didn't know how sound proof the walls of this trailer she was living in were. The last thing she wanted was for Craig to get into trouble, because she'd already decided they needed to do this again.

By the time her spasms slowed, Craig was breathing hard from laboring above her. His stroke quickened, until he pulled out of her. He dropped his head and, groaning into the pillow next to her head, came against her leg.

Still panting, he rolled to one side. He glanced down at the sticky mess on her. "Sorry about that."

She laughed. "Don't apologize."

"You have a towel or something?" he asked.

She waved one boneless arm in the direction of the desk. "Wet wipes are over there."

He rolled off the bed and stood to retrieve the package, tearing into it as he walked back toward her across the narrow space.

"Wet wipes. I'm impressed. You sure you haven't deployed before?" His lips quirked up in a smile.

"I googled what to pack for the Middle East."

He laughed at that, which broke a bit of the awkwardness as he cleaned the remains of their lovemaking off her leg.

After tossing the package back on the desk and the used wipes into the trash bin, he bent to reach toward the pile of his clothes on the floor.

She felt her heart clench. Maybe they wouldn't be repeating what they'd just done.

Bracing herself for the answer, she asked, "Are you leaving?"

Pants in hand, he said, "Not unless you want me

to go."

"No."

"Good." He smiled.

She watched as he turned his tangled clothes right side out and draped them neatly on the back of the chair, ready to be put back on in a moment's notice. He repeated the same with her clothes.

Smiling at his neatness, she said, "Since we don't have to be anywhere until seven hundred hours A.M., I definitely want you to stay."

He laughed. "You can just say zero-seven-hundred. There's no A.M. or P.M. required, since it's a twenty-four hour clock."

She reached out to grab his hand and pulled him back onto the bed. After he'd leaned back on the narrow bunk next to her, she crawled on top of him until she was straddling his hard, naked body.

"You can correct my military speak or we can have sex again. Your choice."

His lips twitched with a smile. "Seven hundred A.M. it is then."

He flipped her over effortlessly and then those lips were occupied doing other tantalizing things to her that she wouldn't mind lasting until the A.M..

CHAPTER TWENTY-FIVE

Banging nearby startled Mary Elizabeth out of her sleep, but didn't wake her up enough to be able to comprehend what was happening.

The same wasn't true of Craig. He was up and on his feet in seconds and dressed even faster.

"Stay here," he said before he yanked open her door and stepped outside, closing it behind him.

Awake now, she jumped out of bed and pulled on her pants and shirt without benefit of underwear or bra.

Dressed good enough for now, she moved to the door and pressed her ear against it.

Bits and pieces of conversation reached her ears. She recognized Craig's voice, but couldn't identify who the other speaker was, other than that he was male.

The words *car bomb* and *eyewitnesses* stood out from among the rest of the muffled exchange, but not much else.

A knock had her jumping back. She pulled the door open and Craig stepped in.

He closed the door behind him. "I'm so sorry but I gotta go."

"Where? What's happening?"

He pressed his lips together but finally said, "There was a car bomb nearby. Civilian American journalists were hit. There were casualties. The locals are tired of the fighting so they reported who was responsible and where they'd gone. It's seems once again my unit is the closest. They've called us in to dispatch with the threat."

"Are you supposed to be telling me this?"

He tipped his head to the side. "Probably not."

"Than why are you?"

"Because I trust you not to repeat it to anyone now or later when you're home. And because after last night, I think you deserve an explanation of why I'm leaving you again."

"It sounds dangerous."

He pulled her close and pressed a kiss to her mouth. "I gotta go. I'll be back as soon as I can. Stay safe while I'm gone and do whatever those Delta guys tell you to do, okay?"

"Okay." She held on to her composure until, after one more backward glance, he closed the door behind him. Then the tears of fear crept into her eyes.

This was not the first time he'd gone. He'd come

back to her that time. He'd come back to her this time too. She had to believe that.

Sleep wasn't going to happen. Not now. She checked the time. It was almost time to get up anyway. She got dressed the right way and even put on her flak jacket like she was supposed to.

Given that, she figured it was okay if she walked to the dining hall alone. She knew the way and it wasn't that far.

After getting there safely, she was just pouring herself a cup of questionable coffee and deciding if she should try to choke down some breakfast when a man stepped up next to her.

"Professor Smith?"

Since she still couldn't decipher ranks, she couldn't address him by his, so she just said, "Yes, that's me."

"Can you come with me, please?"

It was way too early to leave for the Institute, so she assumed this guy wasn't her escort. After all of Craig's warnings to not go anywhere alone she started to worry. Who was this guy? Where was he taking her?

She put down the cup of coffee she held precariously in her hand. With a calmness she didn't think she possessed, she asked, "Why?"

"I don't know. My commander asked I find you and bring you to him. I tried your trailer first and then here."

She glanced around. People on base were starting to wake and filter in to the dining hall, making her feel less isolated. More confident that if she got really scared, she could yell for help.

"Okay." Maybe Grant was asking for her? He was the only commander she knew personally. Maybe it was about her escort while Craig was gone.

Without further discussion he led her to another building and into an office, but the man behind the desk wasn't Grant or anyone else she knew.

Once her escort had left, the stranger behind the desk addressed her. "Professor Smith, I'm afraid you're needed back home at the university."

She frowned. How could that be? They'd already found a replacement for her for the end of the semester. "I don't understand."

"We're going to need you to pack your things. There's a transport heading back to the States in two hours and there's space for you on it."

She didn't want a spot on the transport. She wanted to stay here with Craig and work. "But the Iraqi Institute—"

"Will be informed of the change of plans."

"Is Grant Milton here?" she asked in a last ditch effort to get at least an explanation if not have this horrible new plan changed.

"No, ma'am."

That made sense. If Craig's team had to leave then their commander would have gone as well, not that she knew anything about the inner workings of the military. Right now, that was abundantly clear as this newest order confused the hell out of her.

She didn't understand the change but without Craig or Grant she had no allies here. Panicked, she was starting to feel very alone in Iraq.

Maybe it would be better, safer, if she did go home. But the thought of leaving twisted her insides. Not that her wishes mattered anyway. It was very obvious that, like it or not, she was being ordered to leave.

"Okay. I'll pack." She sighed. "Where should I go for the transport?"

She was so thrown, so upset, she wasn't even sure she could find her way back to her trailer from here, let alone find the plane she was supposed to be on.

"Don't worry about that. O'Brian will go with you and bring you to where you need to be."

This was really happening and there wasn't a damn thing she could do about it. Her work life. Her love life. Everything was upside down. Just when she was starting to feel moderately normal and take back her life, the rug had been yanked out from under her. Just as she'd started to be happy to be alive again, the sadness and the pain settled back in her chest.

Just when her iced over heart had begun to thaw she was right back where she'd been almost a year ago. And she'd only been with Craig a couple of days. They weren't in a relationship. And he hadn't even ended it, the military had.

What the hell would she feel like if they had been together longer? If he had broken it off after they'd been dating a while? She couldn't even imagine the pain. No, actually she could imagine it and it would be devastating. It already was . . .

CHAPTER TWENTY-SIX

"What do you mean she's gone?" Craig asked.

Grant lifted one brow and Craig realized he should have tempered the question a bit. "The assignment's over. We tracked the Russians all the way back to the homeland so it's pointless to keep her here."

"So we're going home too then?"

"No. The team stays here."

Craig wanted to ask more but he figured he was already pressing his luck with Grant.

"Anything else?" Grant asked, looking amused.

"Do we know that she got home safely?" Craig couldn't help asking one last question.

Grant dipped his head. "Yes. We know she got safely on a plane in Virginia headed for Vegas. After that, she's on her own."

"Okay. Thank you."

"Move your stuff into the tent with the team and then get some rest, Dawson. I have a feeling things are going to pick up here."

"Yes, sir." After that comment Craig's hopes of leaving Iraq anytime soon went out the window.

Likely they'd be joining in the fight for Mosul. ISIS was being forced back slowly but surely, but the battle for the city still raged on. And if that were the case, there was something he needed to do before he entered into a door to door, close quarters combat scenario.

He needed to call Mary Elizabeth. He'd taken barely a step toward the recreation building when he realized he still didn't have her cell number.

But he did know where she worked.

Would she be back at her desk already?

He'd been gone one very long week, so she might well be. Taxing his brain he figured out what day of the week it was and what time it would be in Vegas and decided it was worth a shot.

Hopping on an available computer, he searched and found the telephone number for the university and for her department. Using that number, he waited his turn for the phone and then placed the call.

When the switchboard answered, he said, "Professor Mary Elizabeth Smith's office, please."

"One moment."

His heart thundered as he heard the ringing on the line as he was connected to her office. Even if she didn't answer, he could leave a message.

And if she did—then he was going to tell her how he felt about her because after all they'd been through together, even over such a short time, it felt long overdue.

"Hello?"

"Mary. It's Craig."

She hesitated. "Where are you?"

"Still in Iraq."

He heard her blow out a big breath. "They made me leave."

"I know. I'm sorry I wasn't here. I didn't know command was planning that. I didn't find out until when we got back today." He paused but she remained silent, so he continued, "I wanted to tell you something. I know it will be a challenge with me over here for awhile and you there, but I want to give us a try."

She didn't respond.

"Mary? Did I lose you?" It wouldn't be the first time the connection dropped while he was in the middle of a conversation. The only difference is he was usually talking to his mother at the time instead of the woman he was falling in love with.

"I'm here."

She might be there but she didn't sound on board with his suggestion.

"Did you hear what I said? About us?"

"I heard."

This wasn't going exactly as he'd planned. He forced out a laugh. "I'm willing to do the work, but you gotta give me something here."

"I—I can't. Craig, thank you for everything, but

I just can't."

The line went dead for real this time but not before he heard what she'd said, and the tears in her voice.

Stunned, he put down the receiver. What the hell had happened between the time he'd left her and now? He didn't know and as long as he was here, he had no way of finding out.

Crap.

CHAPTER TWENTY-SEVEN

"Come out with us." Amanda repeated herself for what had to be the third time on this phone call alone.

"I don't feel like it."

"But it'll be fun."

No, it wouldn't be fun and going out to a bar where there were men certainly wouldn't make her feel better. A month after her last ill-fated experiment of letting a man back into her life and she was still fighting the pain and depression.

"But—"

"Um, I'm getting another call. I'll call you back." Mary Elizabeth cut off her friend with the lie and hung up the phone.

She felt bad about it but she just couldn't deal with her well meaning friend right now. It was challenging enough to get out of bed each day. Truth be told, some days she didn't even manage that.

Mary consciously drew in a deep breath and let it out slowly. On the days that she had to remind herself to breathe, she knew she was in no shape to socialize. Not on the phone and definitely not out on the town.

Wiping away the tear that had snuck out of her eye, she sniffed in one more big breath and tried to stop feeling sorry for herself and how pitiful her life was now that the darkness had descended over her again.

Weekends were always bad. Tomorrow would be better. At least when she was working her mind was occupied. She'd drug herself with a sleeping pill early tonight and wake up in the morning ready for a new workweek.

It was how she'd made it through most of last year after Rob had left, and how she'd made it through the weeks since her return from Iraq.

Blowing out a breath, she moved to the kitchen. Maybe some herbal tea would help. That and watching a sappy movie for some escapism would kill the time until she could go to sleep.

A knock on the door had her heart falling. Had Amanda finally given up on the phone and just come over? She didn't have it in her to do this right now.

She considered hiding and pretending she wasn't home when the next knock was followed by a very familiar, very male voice saying, "Mary. It's

Craig."

Frozen in place by hearing the one voice she didn't think she'd hear again, she had to knock herself out of the shocked stupor to move toward the door.

She was so grateful he was alive and safely back from Iraq she couldn't leave him standing out there in the hallway. Unlocking the door, she pulled it open and saw the man she never thought she'd see again.

He looked good as he said, "Hi."

In her yoga pants and a slightly stained long sleeved T-shirt, she didn't look quite so good. "Hi."

"Can I come in?"

"Sure." Knowing it was a bad idea she stepped back and let him come in anyway.

"It's good to see you."

"Thanks." Forcing a laugh, she glanced down at herself and assumed he was lying.

"Mary, I want to talk about us."

"Craig, there is no us."

"Why can't there be?" he asked.

"Because there just can't."

"That's not an answer."

She let out a breath. He was right. He deserved more. "I thought I could do it. Just have sex with you and not get attached, but I can't."

"Good." His eyes widened. "I *want* you to get attached because I already am."

"You don't understand. I can't be with you."

"Why not?"

"Because I can't go through the pain of the end

of another relationship. I won't be able to handle it when you leave."

He shook his head. "But I won't leave."

"You don't know that. You're young." She glanced up at the ceiling and laughed at herself. "God, I'm afraid to even ask you how young you are. And I definitely should have asked long before I had sex with you. Before I got attached to you."

"What does age have to do with anything?"

"Because you don't know how you'll feel in the future about me. About us."

"I'm doing my best to not be insulted that you think I'm too immature to know how I feel."

"I didn't say that."

Craig took a step forward. "It doesn't matter how young or old I am. I know exactly how I feel. I love you."

The words affected her. Her eyes filled with tears that spilled over onto her cheeks. "It doesn't matter what you feel. What you believe. Because you might not have a choice. With your job, you can get sent away. You could die."

She knew he couldn't argue with her on that since he'd been sent away twice just in the short time they'd been together.

"Mary, we all can die and you know that. This isn't about my age or my job."

"You're right. It's about me but that doesn't change anything. The man who stayed with me for eight years and promised me a future left me. I can't get hurt like that again."

"Whoever did that to you was a spineless,

shameful, sorry excuse for a man. Don't let him change you. He doesn't deserve to have power over you or your future."

"I know. I'm just . . . I'm so broken." Her tears fell freely now.

"Not all men are like him. *I'm* not like him."

"I wish I could believe that."

"You can."

"I can't. I'm scared."

"I told you in Iraq, being scared is okay. You just have to figure out how to deal with it. It's being afraid to live because you're too scared that's not okay."

Craig wasn't unaffected by her tears. She saw his eyes go glassy as he touched her cheek.

"Give me a chance. No, you know what?" He shook his head. "Give *yourself* a chance. Give *us* a chance. Don't do it for me. Do it for you."

She smiled through her tears. "You're awfully wise for being so young."

Craig cocked a brow. "I'm getting older every day. And wiser. And more in love with you." He moved in closer as she watched him warily. "And you're strong and smart and independent. Whether you realize it or not, I know you don't need to be with anyone to be complete. But that doesn't mean you're not allowed to want to be with someone. With me."

His words brought on a renewed gush of tears as her mind spun. She was miserable without him. She couldn't possibly hurt worse so why not give them a chance?

Maybe happiness was worth the gamble.

Craig drew in a breath and looked as if he was resigning himself for her to shoot him down again.

She didn't. Instead, she wrapped her arms around his neck as she pressed her lips to his in a short but passionate kiss.

She drew back just enough to say, "Okay."

"Okay?" he asked, looking surprised.

She let out a laugh. "Yes, I want to be with you and give us a chance. And I love you too."

"Thank god." He let out a huge breath and lifted her into the air.

She squealed as her feet left the ground. When he finally put her down she said, "What do we do now?"

He still lived on the east coast and worked all over the world. And she still lived and worked in Nevada.

Love was one thing but geography was another.

"We'll figure that out. Together. Okay?" he asked.

Somehow, as his gaze held hers, the distance didn't seem to matter.

She nodded, betting that if anyone could solve their problems, it would be him.

EPILOGUE

"The frigging media is making up stories again." A man farther down the bar tossed his cell phone down next to his drink. He swiveled on the barstool to face the man seated next to him. "Now they're saying they uncovered another 'leaked' story."

"What this time?" the other man asked after a derogatory snort.

"Russian spies."

"Living here in the US? Like in that TV show?" the speaker's drinking buddy asked.

"I think they already claimed to find that a coupla' years ago. But no, this article says these supposed spies are in the Middle East monitoring coalition troop movements."

"I don't know why you keep reading that shit."

"Can't help it. The shit keeps coming up in the feed on my cell."

As the conversation near them continued, Craig could feel Mary Elizabeth getting antsier by the moment.

"Don't . . ." he said softly to her.

She spun her head to look at him, wide-eyed. "But—"

"No." He widened his own eyes in warning.

She pressed her lips together, looking unhappy. "I just don't understand."

He debated whether to continue this conversation here or cut her off until they could talk alone.

She continued before he had a chance to decide. "If we know the truth, why can't we share it? Why gather this intel if we never use it?"

No matter how adorable he found her use of the word *intel*, or how her pout made him want to kiss her lips right there in the bar, he had to shut her down.

"It's what we do. We gather it, then someone higher up the chain of command uses it as they see fit. That's not our job."

She let out a huff and grabbed her drink to down another swallow, only reinforcing the opinion he already had—Mary Elizabeth was too inquisitive for her own good and he loved her even more for it.

Thank goodness her involvement in the team's uncover assignment in Iraq was over.

She should be pleased her short time there had yielded the knowledge they needed. He'd told her that much, but every once in a while over the past six months since the op had ended her displeasure in the military's use, or lack of use, of the intel reared its head. Like now.

Based on what knowledge they'd gathered in Erbil, and aided by the tracking device Craig had slipped into the head Russian's jacket at the Institute on day one before the three men had high-tailed it out of there, someone above Craig's pay grade had been tracking the elusive team of "experts".

He didn't know specifics, as he'd told Mary Elizabeth that wasn't his job, but Grant had hinted that the movements of the so-called experts alluded to them researching a lot more than artifacts.

Mary knew a very tiny bit of the story, but not the whole thing. Knowing she was being kept in the dark was enough to make her a very unhappy camper these past months.

With a hand on the back of her neck, he pulled her closer and pressed a kiss to her mouth. It was his favorite way to alleviate her foul mood. Or *one* of his favorite ways anyway.

He smiled when he finally released her lips. "Stop pouting on my birthday."

That brought on an eye roll from her. "I know. I should be grateful. Today, and for the next six months until my birthday, we're only seven years apart in age instead of eight."

"You know we have a deal about discussing our ages," he reminded her.

If she brought up the subject of their age difference he got to request anything he wanted from her.

He considered what was still on his bucket list. Sex at the beach maybe? She'd been fighting him on that one.

She frowned. "You brought it up so it doesn't count."

"Fine." He drew in a breath and let it out, pretending to be disappointed. "Anyway, tell me what dusty old things you worked on today."

Work at the Institute in Erbil had done more than provide them access to the Russian team. It had also shown Mary Elizabeth a new career path. Craig had no complaints that her path had brought her to the East Coast and closer to him.

Her eyes lit up with excitement, as they always did when she discussed her work. "It's amazing. Craig, just the things they have in storage at the Smithsonian are enough to take my breath away."

His lips twitched. "You really do enjoy storage rooms, don't you? Perhaps that's someplace to add to my bucket list."

Though he'd have to check the storage room for security cameras first. He didn't want to get her fired from her new job.

She cocked one brow up at that. "You're too young to have a bucket list, sexual or other."

He grinned wide. "And that time *you* brought up my age so . . ."

Sighing, she wrapped both arms around his neck. "You're lucky I love you."

Pulling her closer, he said, "Yeah, I am. Very."

Hot SEALs

Night with a SEAL
Saved by a SEAL
SEALed at Midnight
Kissed by a SEAL
Protected by a SEAL
Loved by a SEAL
Tempted by a SEAL
Wed to a SEAL
Romanced by a SEAL
Rescued by a Hot SEAL
Betting on a Hot SEAL
Escape with a Hot SEAL

For more titles by Cat visit CatJohnson.net

ABOUT THE AUTHOR

Cat Johnson is a top 10 *New York Times* bestseller and the author of the *USA Today* bestselling Hot SEALs series. She writes contemporary romance featuring sexy alpha heroes and is known for her unique marketing. She has sponsored pro bull riders, owns a collection of camouflage and western wear for book signings, and has used bologna to promote romance novels.

Never miss a new release or a sale again. Join Cat's inner circle at catjohnson.net/news.

CPSIA information can be obtained
at www.ICGtesting.com
Printed in the USA
BVOW03s1759020717
488350BV00001B/1/P